I0682643

don't let the revolution leave you behind . . .

Jeff VanderMeer Liz Williams **Jeffrey Ford**
Catherynne M. Valente **Alex Irvine** Leslie What
Robert Freeman Wexler Hal Duncan **Lisa Mantchev** Richard Bowes **Jason Erik Lundberg**
Rachel Swirsky **Alan DeNiro** Chris Roberson
Christopher Rowe Charles Coleman Finlay **Marly Youmans** Scott William Carter

They've already joined, what are you waiting for?

http://www.electricvelocipede.com

Weird Tales ®

JULY-AUGUST 2008

SUBSCRIBE AT WWW.WEIRDTALESMAGAZINE.COM

WEIRD TALES was the *first* storytelling magazine devoted explicitly to the realm of the **dark and fantastic.**

Founded in 1923, WEIRD TALES provided a literary home for such diverse wielders of the imagination as **H.P. Lovecraft** (creator of Cthulhu), **Robert E. Howard** (creator of Conan the Barbarian), **Margaret Brundage** (artistic godmother of goth fetishism), and **Ray Bradbury** (author of *The Illustrated Man* and *Something Wicked This Way Comes*).

Today, O wondrous reader of the 21st century, we continue to seek out that which is most weird and unsettling, for your own edification and alarm.

FICTION

EDITORIAL & CREATIVE DIRECTOR Stephen H. Segal FICTION EDITOR Ann VanderMeer
CONTRIBUTING EDITORS Scott Connors, Amanda Gannon, Elizabeth Genco, Darrell Schweitzer
EDITOR EMERITUS George H. Scithers EDITORIAL ASSISTANTS Krystal Garvin,
Tessa Kum CONTRIBUTING ARTISTS Victoria Alexandrova, Steven Archer,
Paul Bielaczyc, Ira Marcks, Doreen Salcher, Simone Van Den Berg

PUBLISHER John Gregory Betancourt
ADVERTISING SALES Evelyn Kriete ASSISTANT TO THE PUBLISHER Renee Farrah

All writers of such stories are prophets

FEATURES

POETRY

HELLBOY: THE WILD HUNT / DARK HORSE COMICS

DEPARTMENTS

COVER ILLUSTRATION | **Jason Levesque** | stuntkid.com

VOL. 63, NO. 3 | **Issue 350**

WEIRD TALES ® is published 6 times a
year by Wildside Press, LLC. Postmaster
and others: send all changes of address
and other subscription matters to Wildside Press, 9710 Traville Gateway Dr.
#234, Rockville MD 20850–7408. Single
copies, $6.99 in U.S.A. & possessions; $10
by first class mail elsewhere. Subscrip-
tions: 6 issues $24 in U.S.A. & posses-
sions; $45 elsewhere, in U.S. funds.
Single-copy orders should be addressed to
WEIRD TALES at the address above.
Copyright © 2008 by Wildside Press, LLC.
All rights reserved; reproduction prohib-
ited without prior permission. Typeset &
printed in the United States of America.
WEIRD TALES ® is a registered trademark owned by Weird Tales, Limited.

The eyrie

A VIEW FROM UNEARTHLY HEIGHTS

On Metamorphoses

BY ANN VANDERMEER

I'VE BEEN THINKING a lot about change lately. Especially since it's an election year, and each candidate professes to be bringing change. That's all I'm hearing. "Something's gotta change." "I am the candidate of change." "We can't keep going along as we have been or death and destruction will soon be raining down upon us." Well, maybe that last one is a bit extreme. But you get the point.

Change is inevitable. We can't escape it no matter what we do. And although some of us embrace change, we shouldn't embark on it solely for the purpose of change.

I work with this concept every day. In my other life as a consultant, I walk into businesses of all types and point out where change is needed. Most of them balk at it. They fight me and tell me all the reasons why they can't change. But the reason I'm there is because their status quo has proven unsustainable. I've been called in to effect a change so their companies can run more efficiently and yes, more profitably. I'm the one they bring in when the pain of *not* changing is greater than the change. I guess you can call me an agent of change; just don't nominate me for elected office. I have *way* too many skeletons in the closet.

I saw a movie last year that illustrates this whole issue of change very well. *Kinky Boots* is based on a true story about a man who inherits his father's very traditional shoe factory in North England. The business is failing; no one seems to want the same old same old shoes anymore. After a trip to London, Charlie Price has a chance encounter with a drag queen and comes up with the wacky idea to make boots for this under-served part of society. Needless to say, this change is met with great resistance both from the employees of the factory and Charlie's girlfriend. But Charlie takes a chance. He goes for it and eventually gets support from those around him. He is able to turn the factory around and we have a happy ending.

We all generally want to be comfortable; our tendency is to want things to remain as they are. But sometimes that just isn't possible. I've found it's important to help people ease into the scarier transitions, so they have time to see how a given change can be a good thing. Well, that's a great concept in the business world — but how does it fit with fiction?

The stories in this issue are all about change. In Kelly Barnhill's "The Stone-Hearted Queen," a young girl is transformed into a stone. Ramsey Shehadeh shows us how a mobster handles a corporeal make-over upon traveling into purgatory in "How I Got Here." Norman Spinrad explores in "Right You Are If You Say You Are" how much power one person can have when he can become anything he wants purely by thinking it. Check out Adam Corbin Fusco's "Bel-air Plaza," where a strip mall tries to change but can't escape its own true nature. In "The Difficulties of Evolution," Karen Heuler shows us a mother who resists the inevitable. Nick Mamatas proves you can't go home again in "Mainevermontnewhampshiremass." Peter Atwood deals with physical change and the extent to which we're willing to go in "All In." And who can resist a story about star-crossed centipede lovers such as "Ganaranok's Lament" by Rory Steves?

Weird Tales has never been known to maintain the status quo. The fiction in *WT* is supposed to make you uncomfortable, right? It's supposed to

Last month's anniversary feature on **The 85 Weirdest Storytellers of the Past 85 Years** generated a huge response. Turn to page 96 for a sampling of reader reactions — and join the ongoing discussion at **WeirdTalesMagazine.com**!

4 ~ WEIRD TALES ~ July–August 2008

challenge you and make you think. And not by shoving it in your face or ramming it down your throat. Oh, no. That's not the *Weird Tales* way. A weird tale does more than that. It gets under your skin and it becomes part of you. And you become part of it.

So take a ride with us. We're curious to see who *you* become at the end of the journey. ℮

FROM WEIRD READERS

Thrilled To Have Been Thrilled

Your latest issue seems sincerely given over to fearful chillers and, I think, deserves commendations for giving readers the full show. Lately, tales of fright have seemed somewhat out of style, overshadowed by macabre tales of horror, but I like to see a good panic every now and then . . . [like] the October 1927 issue that Robert Bloch said scared him "out of a year of growth." Well, this recent issue put me plenty uptight and had me looking behind me.

As to the magazine's new look, I had been feeling quite satisfied with its traditional appearance and didn't at first like the new [cover] design, but as things have progressed, I think the avant-garde look is quite in keeping with the contents — and is also more sensational than well-fortified tradition. Perhaps we'll be seeing more spectres than ghouls in the magazine, and that is quite all right with me. I assume you'll really be making the reader sit up and take notice! *— John Thiel*

LETTERS TO THE EDITOR

Letters may be emailed to letters@weirdtales.net or snail-mailed to *Weird Tales*, 9710 Traville Gateway Dr. #234, Rockville MD 20850-7408. Letters may be edited for publication.

PSEUDOPOD
the new voice of horror

Wake up each day (or night) to bone-chilling stories from the most talented authors working today, delivered straight to your computer or portable MP3 player.

Eldritch! Sure.

Squamous! Perhaps.

Free? Definitely.

Pseudopod is the world's premier audio horror fiction magazine.

It's professional, unpredictable, disturbing, — and it's

IN YOUR EARS.

PSEUDOPOD
the new voice of horror

Make your morning MONSTROUS.

Listen or subscribe at pseudopod.org

Weirdism

UNDER A BLACK SUN

Culture | BY GEOFFREY H. GOODWIN

EGO LIKENESS PHOTO COURTESY WWW.KYLECASSIDY.COM

D ARK MUSIC AND dark literature share something like the thrill of hearing a dry twig crackle in the woods when you're alone and standing still. They're about following headtrips to brinks of emotion and fatigue. As such, to ask why weird kids, and the weird kids who've grown up to become weird adults, go to a musical event like the BlackSun Festival is to ask why readers enjoy the nightmare logic of the best weird tales.

Fifteen miles outside of New Haven, Connecticut, on the fourteenth of March, giant highway signs alerted travelers they were entering a FOG AREA. Those not scared off by that horror-movie cliché come to life eventually found themselves strolling into New Haven's leading concert venue, Toad's Place, where a scene equal parts *Donnie Darko* and *Pan's Labyrinth* was in full bloom. Five hundred congregants were dressed in funereal ball gowns, occasional white frills, gas masks, goggles, unnaturally-colored dreads, and lots of pierced-heart tattoos — it was as if all of SuicideGirls.com had sprung to three-dimensional life from the computer screen, accidentally covered in a few pieces of clothing. Considering the festival's cyberpunk provenance, that impression wasn't far from the truth.

Named for the virtual nightclub in Neal Stephenson's 1992 dark science-fiction classic *Snow Crash* — which directly inspired today's Web 2.0 world of avatars, widgets, and friendlists — BlackSun originated in Amsterdam as a short-lived nightclub event where an American DJ, Jonathan Kephart, spun the music. That incarnation didn't last long, but Kephart really liked the logo for which he'd paid $200; so, upon returning to the U. S., he repurposed the name for a festival that would feature some of the most atmospheric new gothic-type performers of the infant millennium. He looked for a location that would be on a rail line within reach of both Boston and New York, and found New Haven, a city small enough that attendees could walk from venue to venue. Even more importantly, New Haven had the moody character he wanted. Cue the fog.

Running down the roster of performers and exhibitors at this year's BlackSun Festival, it's hard to find one who *doesn't* have a connection to the world of weird fantasy and science fiction. There's Projekt Records founder Sam Rosenthal, a dark-music pioneer for the past 25 years, whose new solo project is called As Lonely As Dave Bowman in reference to the character in *2001*. There's Bloodwire, a boy-girl duo whose gentle melodies belie their name, and whose songwriter Shawn Brice is an avowed H.P. Lovecraft fan. There's electronic balladeer Tom Shear, a.k.a. Assemblage 23, whose repertoire features apocalyptic imagery aplenty and whose favorite author is Chuck Pahlaniuk.

And then there's Ego Likeness, a Baltimore duo comprising the sylphy voice of Donna Lynch and the musical antics of guitarist Steven Archer. Their lyrics are steeped in dark and gloomy imagery and explore alienation, decadence, and dark rituals. Some of their songs slither and smolder, while others veer into jangling triphop. It's no wonder they cite Poe, Gaiman, and Barker as some of their favorite writers; between Lynch's haunting vocals and Archer's hypnotic riffs, the two made their seven p.m. showtime feel like the dead of the night.

Offstage, Lynch and Archer tap into the dark-fantasy culture in other media. The independent horror publisher Raw Dog Screaming released Lynch's poetry collection *Ladies and Other Vicious Creatures* with illustrations by Archer, and her novel *Isabel Burning* will come out in August. Lynch describes the new book as "a love story. Ancient malevolent entities living in quarries, unethical bio-spiritual experiments, twisted relationships, viscera, and ghosts — you know, the usual." Meanwhile, Archer brings a fine-art, gallery-quality approach to surrealistic fantasy art, creating and selling original mixed-media paintings of tortured souls and alien cephalopods. (See "365 Days," below.)

Two weeks after BlackSun, Ego Likeness crossed the lines of disparate media to put in a weekend's work selling books, paintings, and music at the Horrorfind convention at the University of Maryland, where Lynch's luminescent platinum tresses and Archer's bouncy purple dreadlocks seemed as comfortable in a roomful of zombie-movie fans as they had in a club full of dancing goths. "It's really all the same thing," muses Lynch, "just different mediums. That isn't to say that all horror is 'gothy' nor all goth music frightening — but in both subcultures, there's a willingness by the creator and the consumer to venture into darker, unusual places." ℮

BlackSun Festival: www.blacksun-festival.com. **Projekt Records:** www.projekt.com. **Bloodwire:** www.bloodwire.com. **Assemblage 23:** www.assemblage23.com. **Ego Likeness:** www.egolikeness.com.

MORE INFO

365 DAYS OF BLASPHEMOUS HORRORS

As we prepped this issue of *Weird Tales*, Steven Archer (above) showed us a bold new project he'd just started creating: a year-long series of 365 original, *daily* artworks inspired mostly by H.P. Lovecraft's Cthulhu Mythos. We've never seen Lovecraftian art quite like this before — so we're bringing it to you! Visit **WeirdTalesMagazine.com** every single day from now through Memorial Day 2009 and you'll have the chance not only to see the debut of this incredible new horror art, but also to purchase the originals!

WHISPERS *of the* OLD HAG

Nonfiction
BY ERIC SAN JUAN

THE THING WAS made of light and shadow; skeletal, pale, with ribs like talons and deep eager eyes. I did not know the time. Didn't care to know, really. Midnight; 4 a.m.; whatever. How could I care when it stood there, just outside my bedroom door, framed in moonlight and a clinging mist; a malevolent thing, angry and waiting? The time didn't matter. All that mattered was that I was being watched.

I longed to scream, but the sound would not come. A hoarse croak. A gasp of breath. Nothing more. I was silent; immobile; paralyzed.

It's impossible to recall how old I was when it first happened. Twelve. Maybe fourteen. The experience was terrifying, a mix of dread and horror and of being utterly overcome by something alien. The experience was no dream. It was real and true. And it would happen again.

Once, an unseen presence woke me in the night and sat on my chest. I could not see it, but I could feel it perched upon me. As it sat there pressing the air from my lungs, the walls filled with whispers. Most of them were incomprehensible, but at times snatches of words tormented me: accusations, laughter, distant discussion tantalizingly close to being understood. I strained to call to them, to tell them I was trapped, to beg to be released from this unseen prison, but again my voice was frozen.

On another occasion, I could see the presence. A curtain was spread across my doorway, pulled slightly open, and as I awoke from a soft afternoon sleep I saw it, a black shadow pacing back and forth just outside the room. "Who's there?" I called, but no sound came. Again my voice was frozen. Again I could not move. Again the whispers came. Just beyond the curtain they chattered, always on the very edge of understanding.

The visits continued sporadically over the years. A woman I knew, a self-styled fortuneteller, the sort who thinks she knows the secrets of the universe, told me something was happening. That I was breaking through some wall. Some barrier. That maybe, just maybe, it was dangerous.

She wasn't far off the mark. As it turned out, I was treading in territory that had tormented man for all recorded history. I was swimming in the blackest waters of night; grasping at nightmares made real. Yet it was not the journey into otherworldly hells she suggested.

I was suffering from sleep paralysis: a bizarre fluke of consciousness that occurs while on the borderlands of sleep, thrusting the victim into a place between dreaming and waking. A very scary place.

When one enters REM sleep, something called "REM atonia" kicks in, a state during which the body's muscles do not move. You are, in essence, paralyzed. This is perfectly normal. It happens to every sleeper. In the case of sleep paralysis, however, the mind awakens, becomes aware and conscious — *mostly* — even while the body still sleeps. And then come the hallucinations.

The feeling of a presence, almost always malevolent, is common. The feeling of being watched, sometimes of a crushing pressure, is also typical. There is always dread. Always fear. Sometimes unbridled panic. And sometimes voices, barely understandable but tantalizingly recognizable. I've heard people chatting in the next room or just outside my window, familiar voices and alien voices, the voices of loved ones and the voices of strangers. Yet none of them were real.

"Not real" — but for all the terror they brought me, they might as well have been. The foothills between waking and sleep are a harsh place, a landscape of half-seen truths and elusive lies. Tarry too long, dwell upon the seeming realism of the frightening episodes too obsessively — *believe* too much of what you see — and you could find yourself swallowed up by your own mind. This was the danger from which I ran.

I'd left fears of demons behind with childhood. Poltergeists, hauntings, ghosts; sure, the images could provide a chill, but the same could be said for anyone with a vivid imagination. This doesn't mean we really believe in such things. We don't. As a society, we've moved beyond taking such fears seriously. But hang on — because humanity has a new terror of the night. A new presence that comes in the evening and whisks away the unsuspecting. Demons of the modern age. They come from space, drifting out of the sky bathed in cold lights, bringing their emotionless and distant violations with them.

The gray alien — the now-familiar visage of the silent, petite, triangle-faced, giant-eyed extraterrestrial — *that's* today's demonic visitor. Frighteningly inhuman; rendering people helpless; changing the way some live their lives. Alien abduction is a terror many of us believe in. Could sleep paralysis explain these experiences? All the calling cards are there. Waking in the night, unable to move. The feeling of a presence in the room. Losing control of your body. Even a sense that time isn't quite flowing right. Like pieces of some twisted puzzle, it all fits. So if these experiences are simply the result of sleep paralysis, are people investing themselves in the belief that they have been taken by aliens when the real explanation is something much less sinister?

A sleep terror strikes in Paul Bielaczyc's "Nightmare."

It wouldn't be the first time sleep paralysis has done exactly that. The belief that this experience is something more than a biological quirk in the body's sleep mechanism has been around as long as man has feared the night. In *Romeo and Juliet*, Shakespeare makes mention of "the Old Hag." The Old Hag is a demon of the night right out of foggy old myths, describing an entity — whether a witch, demon, or spirit does not matter — that sits on its victim, rendering them unable to move and making it difficult to breath. Sound familiar?

The myth of the Incubus, a demon which lies upon sleeping women in order to violate them, may have sprung from the same source. Peer at the mosaic of language and things begin to fall into place. The Old English word for the Incubus was *maire*, which means "one who oppresses or crushes." In German, it is *mare*. And from these we get "night *mare*," or simply *nightmare*. What it all means is: "A per-

fectly normal sleep thing that scares the screaming holy fuck out of us."

I recalled this one recent evening when, after having drifted off to sleep, I awoke, unable to move. Outside my bedroom window were voices. My father, I think, and my wife. Others, too. I could not understand them. And then something malevolent came into the room. And stood at the foot of the bed. And watched.

This experience was nothing new, not for me and not for mankind. From restless spirits to space-faring entities, from the Incubus to the gray alien, from *Romeo and Juliet* to *Close Encounters of the Third Kind*, we can cast our fears in a new guise. We can give it a new name and a new face. Yet ultimately, the haunts of our evening remain the same: a hiccup of sleep and a lack of understanding. Once I understood that, it was an easy enough demon to exorcize. I needed neither holy water nor holy man. No scientists; no laser beams; no necklace of garlic. Just some understanding . . . and the terror was no more. Sometimes, that's all the exorcism you need. ℮

The Library

A DEN OF INFINITY

Books | BY SCOTT CONNORS

The British Film Institute recently released the 1950 film adaptation of Gerald Kersh's novel *Night and the City* on DVD: www.bfi.org.uk.

THE WORLD, THE FLESH, AND THE DEVIL by Gerald Kersh (Ash-Tree Press, $47.50)

Gerald Kersh was a hugely prolific and popular writer who might well have been to the Britain of the mid-twentieth century what Rudyard Kipling and H.G. Wells were to the late nineteenth. He wrote in 1943: "You may like sordid realism or wild fantasy, sticky romance or spicy sex drama, horror or rosebuds, love or hate, misery or joy — the greatest composer of stories is life itself, and the greatest teller of stories is the man who clings faithfully to life as it is lived." Kersh wrote in all these genres, faithfully recording life as he saw it — but his vision of humanity and of man's position in the universe was perhaps as bleak as that of H.P. Lovecraft, echoes of whom may be heard in one of Kersh's best known tales, "Men Without Bones."

Kersh was a product of the popular journalism of his time, and many of the stories we find in the new collection *The World, The Flesh, and The Devil* are noteworthy for their treatment of contemporary issues. For instance, "One Case in a Million" appears to have been inspired by hangman Albert Pierrepoint, who was reviled after his participation in the controversial execution of murderess Ruth Ellis. Several of the stories here are allegories, but more interesting are the satires, such as the prescient "Comrade Death," with its chilling prediction of the effects of nuclear warfare. "The Epistle of

Simple Simon" is a rather unsubtle swipe at how far blind faith may deviate from what has become known recently as "the reality-based community" — and is reminiscent of a scene in Martin Scorsese's *The Last Temptation of Christ,* though of course Kersh's story predates it. Some of the science-fiction stories have been overtaken by history, as in "Note on Danger B," which speculates on some possible effects of breaching the sound barrier. But others, like "The Brighton Monster," use some of the same background to make powerful observations about alienation and cultural relativism.

The sense of being cast adrift in a meaningless universe is a common and powerful motif in Kersh's work; indeed, it is implied in the very title of his first (suppressed) book, *Jews Without Jehovah.* This is literally the case in both "The Brighton Monster" and "Neither Man Nor Dog." The latter story is one of several Kersh wrote about a ferocious Russian named Adze who, as he is depicted in "The Wolf Dies in Silence," might have given Robert E. Howard's Conan the Cimmerian lessons in toughness. Adze is a Hobbesian character living in a state of nature without any of the gentler emotions. "Wolf, Wolf" demonstrates his almost sociopathic practicality and lack of sentiment. "Kannibalsky" is an ironic commentary on how closely the saint and the sinner may coexist in each of us — and how disquieting it might be for the idealist to confront this coexistence. The only time Adze shows any apparent humanity is in "Neither Man Nor Dog," a confirmation of John Donne's assertion "No man is an island" that   >>>

continued on page 12

Comics | BY NICK MAMATAS

THE DRIFTING CLASSROOM
VOL. 1 by Kaou Umezu
(Viz Media, $9.99)

The manga boom in the U.S. can be difficult to navigate. Not for teens — they're natural aesthetic explorers — but for adult readers, the five or six new shelves of unfamiliar new comic books that have materialized in most chain bookstores over the past few years tend to be intimidating. Where to begin? Try Kazuo Umezu's *The Drifting Classroom*. The eleven-volume series, originally published in the early 1970s, is the unnerving story of an elementary school that finds itself transported . . . somewhere else. Young Sho, an immature sixth-grader, yells at his mother one morning and declares that he is never coming home. Inexplicably his wish comes true when an earthquake hits and the outside world falls away. What's left is only the social pressure-cooker of the school, the >>>

continued on page 13

"It ain't too cool bein' stuck on an island with some space shot who thinks he's King o' the Zombies or some goddamn thing."

KING OF THE ZOMBIES

A SCREENPLAY BY
RICK HUTCHINS

Author of
The RH Factor

Available at Amazon.com
and other online booksellers

TRIP THE URBAN FANTASTIC

"Variety, along with a willingness to publish new and established writers alike, helps explain PAPER CITIES' considerable appeal... ambitious and entertaining... a delightful and absorbing read."
-Jeff VanderMeer for PUBLISHERS WEEKLY

Edited by Ekaterina Sedia

Forrest Aguirre   Vylar Kaftan
Hal Duncan   Mike Jasper
Richard Parks   Ben Peek
Cat Rambo   Kaaron Warren
Jay Lake   Darin Bradley
Greg van Eekhout   Jenn Reese
Cat Sparks   David Schwartz
Steve Berman   Anna Tambour
Stephanie Campisi   Barth Anderson
Mark Teppo   Catherynne M. Valente
Paul Meloy   Foreword by Jess Nevins

PAPER CITIES
AN ANTHOLOGY OF URBAN FANTASY

ISBN: 978-0-9796246-0-5, 288 pages, 6"x9", $14.95 US

www.sensesfivepress.com

BOOKS, FROM PAGE 10 >>> simultaneously manages to deliver a deliciously misanthropic subtext. We might detect a similar cynical view of man's brutish nature in "Corporal Cuckoo," a tale of an immortal who fails to make the best use of his condition. Ambrose Bierce, one of the best-known cynics of our era, is the protagonist of the Edgar Award-winning tale "The Oxoxoco Bottle," wherein Kersh manages to express simultaneously a cynicism about human motives and a sense of man's helplessness before blind chance.

Kersh did write some more or less conventional weird tales. "The Gentleman All in Black" is a fine variation on the theme of the deal with the Devil and "The White-washed Room" an excellent ghost story, while "Miracle of the Winged Rescue" is a fantasy that would have fit in well into John W. Campbell's classic magazine *Unknown Worlds*. But Kersh's forte was definitely the *conte cruel*, as exemplified in the horrific "Crooked Bone." He displays a deft hand in building his narrative towards the final payoff, which is both foreshadowed by the described events yet still manages to come as a shock.

Kersh was an extremely versatile writer — yet, ironically, that very protean virtuosity made it difficult for his work to survive his death, due to a perception by publishers that it would be difficult to market. He's not the first author whose ouevre has succumbed to the confounding brilliance of its own interstitiality; classic *Weird Tales* favorite Henry Kuttner, for instance, has posthumously been in much the same boat. But all literary resurrections must begin somewhere — so we can hope that, now that Ash-Tree Press has brought us *The World, The Flesh, and The Devil*, there may be future volumes to come collecting more "fantastical writings" of Gerald Kersh.

TO SUBMIT BOOKS FOR REVIEW:

Fiction: *please address to Scott Connors, 4277 Larson Street #52, Marysville CA 95901.* **Nonfiction, comics, weird art/music, etc**: *please address to Weird Tales, Attn: Reviews, 9710 Traville Gateway Drive #234, Rockville MD 20850-7408.*

COMICS, FROM PAGE 11 >>> incompetent-to-sadistic teachers, and hints of what has happened to the rest of the planet.

The Drifting Classroom is not a subtle series. The two-page splashes of the chasm where the school once stood and of the twisting desert landscape to where it has been transported hit the very edge of what can be expressed by ink on digest-sized pages. To calm the students from panicking, a teacher grabs a child and attacks him with a shard of glass from his own broken spectacles. A few pages later, the kid is revealed as the teacher's own son. The principal comes to after being brained by a burglar; when he staggers in to the main office and declares that the faculty pay packets are missing, the teachers can only laugh at him. And while the upper grades worry about their parents and how to retain their composure for the good of the school, the third-graders tie up their teacher and one of the kids makes a break for it.

Over the course of eleven books, Sho emerges as a leader of the students (which proves necessary after his teacher goes mad) and much more is learned about the uncanny landscape to which the school is exiled. There are giant insect attacks and female gangs, plagues and serial killers. Most disturbing of all is the attention paid to detail; the kids are never depicted as anything other than kids, with art that would not be out of place in some 1970s-era Japanese Dick-and-Jane basal reader. The haircuts and ankle socks alone are to die for — and many of the characters do just that.

A whole new culture of comic books was suddenly and inexplicably transported to American shopping malls; for those wanting to pick their way through its world, *The Drifting Classroom* is an excellent place to start.

Find more book reviews in our
SUMMER READING WEIRDUCOPIA
starting on page 80!

PERFECTING THE MASQUERADE

MERIMASK | www.merimask.etsy.com

Concealing your face isn't difficult. Doing so while revealing something of the essential character beneath is another matter entirely — and *that* is what great masks are all about. That's where Andrea Tognetti of Merimask comes in. Each of her mysterious facepieces is constructed of a single piece of cut, carved, and formed top-grain leather. All are unique, hand-tooled, and painted with meticulous attention to detail; Merimask pieces have been featured at performances by Cirque du Soleil. But while the artistry may be gallery-quality — and, indeed, Tognetti's work has hung in exhibits around the nation — these three-dimensional fantasies are durable and fully intended to be worn. So go ahead, choose a second face: blue wolf, scarlet dragon, Green Man, Anubis. For the truly weird and unique, Tognetti does accept custom commissions . . . ℮

HARVEY PELICAN & CO., Favorite Unlikely Supply House on Earth, Ipswich.

ASSORTED ANATOMY.......
FOR EACH AND EVERY OCCASION

No. 2491

TOP A "FRESH FACE" LOOK

HAVE PERFECT GLASSES

HOW ABOUT THE PERFECT EYES?

CAST IRON NECK PLUG page 86.

SNAPPY OPERATOR
No. 2484

PEEVISH MOTORIST
No. 2459

SURLY POET
No. 2466

Windy Silk's STARCH 'N' STIFF
PERFECTLY SUITED FOR KNOTS
BOTH IRISH & MATHMATICAL.

HIGH · GRADE
WRIST PETITE. — A JOINT BENEFIT — HAND MANNISH.
· VARIETY OF · RELEVANT APPLICATION

← GREEN
The FARM HAND

THE DECK · HAND

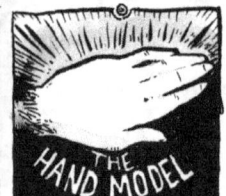

THE HAND MODEL

2 IN STOCK
JILL HANSON *

THE EXTRA ONE

* EXPECT SLIGHT, UNIQUE TAR COLOR.

Harvey's Own Choice

PELICAN

SHIPMENTS

COST

CALL US...
HARVEY PELICAN & Co.
custom services.

SHIPPING RATES SET·BY WEIGHT

I CONSIDER PERSPIRATION, BE READY, HERE COMES THE SUMMER'S REIGN.

DEAR Customer "FRESH FACE"
WHAT IS BEHIND YOUR NEW...
it's
PULSEMAKER'S DRESS COLLAR.

A stylish tube of sulfuric acid, vinegar and water. Bubbles quietly. Providing a subtle jolt. Keeps you up all day.

NOTICE: "FRESH FACE" warranty is VOID if not used in conjunction with Pulsemaker's Dress Collar.

HP & Co

:AS ALWAYS: INCLUDE PAYMENT FOR POST, ICE

Fame

BY K.J. BERGMANN

"Somehow managed to attract a small disturbed
following." — *Jay Griswold, Autobiography III*

Because they took to lurking behind bookcases,
wearing velvet cloaks over their stained armor
instead of sitting in the neat rows of folding chairs,
the word has gotten out to most bookstores
that it would not be a good idea to have me read.

Coffee shops said that my audiences didn't spend
enough on muffins and could make one small house
coffee last three hours, but I knew that it was really
because their insectile hauberks put the regulars right
off their cappuccinos and cherry-vanilla cheesecake.

Cabals of librarians whispered disapprovingly about
the humming along, or, in the case of an especially
rousing poem, the chanting repetition of last lines,
punctuated by sharp blows in unison with the handles
of their pikes. Nor were the torches appreciated.

In public parks, I always seemed to have the wrong
kind of permit, and was charged with everything
from littering to sedition. They arrested me, not my odd
listeners—who for some reason were never asked
for spare change. Nobody minded the missing pigeons.

In order to read where no one would notice my sinister
fans, with a snorkel I waded into a cold, murky river
whose amphibrachic name began with Y — or was it Z?
I recited hastily from my gently dissolving chapbooks
as the wavering shapes began to materialize

and close in.

MORPHEUS TALES

MAGAZINE OF HORROR,
SCIENCE FICTION AND FANTASY

From the creative minds behind

BLACK TEARS MAGAZINE

VIOLENT SPECTRES MAGAZINE

and

MORPHEUS PRESS

MORPHEUS TALES IS A
QUARTERLY MAGAZINE
FEATURING THE HIGHEST
QUALITY FICTION, ARTWORK
AND REVIEWS OF THE
LATEST BOOKS AND FILMS.

www.morpheustales.com
(on myspace at)
www.myspace.com/morpheustales

When Mike Mignola was but a wee lad of ten or twelve years old, he read a book that would change everything. From the moment he closed the covers, he knew what he wanted to do with the rest of his life. The book? Dracula. The inner calling? Monsters.

Mike got to work, pursuing his newfound goal with passion and fervor. His self-imposed training regimen included many trips to Berkeley's used bookstores and countless hours devouring the likes of Lovecraft and Smith, Bloch and Howard. (You know, a Weird Tales who's who.) And folk tales. And classic monster movies. And lots and lots of comics.

Fast-forward a couple of decades. After years of penciling superhero comics for Marvel and DC, the moment Mike had been waiting for had finally arrived: the chance to do his own thing. He took all his literary, folklore, and

Interview | BY ELIZABETH GENCO

Mike Mignola: Hellboy's Dad

pulp-fiction loves and funneled them into his singular new creation: a grizzled, beet-red demon working for the good guys. (Good thing, too, what with that Right Hand Of Doom and all.) Mission accomplished.

The second Hellboy feature film hits theaters in July.

So what have you been up to? Is *Hellboy 2* finished? My work on *Hellboy 2* wrapped up a long time ago. I was only really involved in pre-production, and I made one visit to the set. Which wasn't really work!

What exactly did you do? A few months after the first movie was finished, Guillermo [Del Toro, acclaimed director of *Hellboy* and *Pan's Labyrinth*] and I came up with an original story. I co-plotted; he turned it into the screenplay. I came in for three months on pre-production in LA, and then for a couple of weeks in Budapest. Rough concept stuff.

How did you meet Del Toro in the first place? When he heard that the studio wanted to do a *Hellboy* film, he approached them. Then he and I met and we hit it off instantly. I knew right away that if there was anybody I wanted to see make a *Hellboy* movie, it was certainly going be this guy.

The commentaries on the first film are so much fun to listen to. You two hit it off so well. It's spooky how much we have in common.

He also loves his monsters. Yeah, it's very funny. I was living in Portland at the time and we met for breakfast, courtesy of Dark Horse, my publisher. Afterwards Guillermo and I immediately went off went to the best used bookstore in America, which is in Portland. [*That'd be Powells, of course —ed.*] Then we went back to my apartment and we discovered some crazy similarities. I mean, right down to what books I had on my shelf, and where. I put certain authors together and it makes no logical sense, and yet he was going, "Oh, I put this guy next to that guy too!" It was really pretty weird.

Your stories read like a who's who of mythology, folklore and occultism — you're really quite well-read on this stuff. I admit to having been pleasantly surprised at some of the rather obscure references in *Hellboy*. It's always been my interest, ever since I read *Dracula* as a kid. *Dracula* kind of opened my eyes. I tend to approach it from the folklore and literary sides rather than the big movie monster side. *Dracula* turned me on to that Victorian

era of literature, but also there was a folklore element in that story. It really sent me in two directions: in the literature direction, and the folklore direction.

So ever since then I've been collecting and reading this stuff. And I always knew that if I ever got to that point in comics where I could do whatever I wanted, I'd draw on that material. In fact, before I did *Hellboy*, there were a couple of different folktales I'd planned to adapt into comics and both of them ended up turning into *Hellboy* stories.

So almost from the very beginning, I recognized that Hellboy was a vehicle to do these stories. Unfortunately, if you do a straight adaptation of an English folktale, nobody's going to give a shit. But if you do it wrapped around a character like this, a lot more people are going to pay attention to it.

What draws you into in these stories? Why do you love them so much? It's the weirdness. Especially with folklore, it's just the weirdness — these strange things that defy all logic. Folklore and fairy tale logic is something that Del Toro and I are always making reference to. Where you think, "That seems right, but I don't know why..."

If you read a lot of this material, you'll see certain rhythms and patterns. But part of the rhythm and patterns is things like, "two plus two adds up to a pine tree." How the hell did we get there from here? Things like in a Russian folktale where a cat and a bird warn a guy that this is the time of the year that Baba Yaga will come in the window . . . and count your silverware.

A lot of writers will take a story like that and either change that element, or feel compelled to explain that element. But the beauty of that stuff is that there's no possible explanation for it. Certain things "just happen."

And to think it all started with *Dracula*...! Yeah! It's a very strange thing, but I remember finishing that book or being in the middle of that book and almost making

a conscious decision: "Oh. This is it." I had discovered my "thing." And there was never any straying from the path. I can almost say that since reading *Dracula*, I probably haven't read even a dozen books that don't have monsters in them that weren't required for a class or something.

Okay, so that's an overstatement. But *Dracula* certainly did make me realize what world I was interested in.

And there's some Lovecraft in there too. *Weird Tales* and the pulp magazines introduced me to this other kind of Big Cosmic Horror thing: Lovecraft and the whole circle of Lovecraft guys. And there was just something magical about it. I discovered people like Lovecraft, and learned that all this stuff was published in some magazine called *Weird Tales*, and it was like hearing about this whole other world.

So part of the Lovecraft influence is a real nostalgia for those pulp magazines. But there's also the fact that Lovecraft had this amazing vision of this giant unknowable universe, which is something I've tried to pick up and put in my own stuff. This idea that so much of what we're dealing with is beyond human comprehension.

How do you mean? I hate rules and regulations in supernatural stuff. I hate things like coming up with formulas that say, "If you're bitten by a vampire, after three days you turn into a vampire." That's not in the old folklore, and in my view, as soon as you put rules on things, it becomes science fiction. Sometimes Lovecraft almost veers into sci-fi, but generally his worlds are so huge that they become unknowable. There's a mystery. I've tried to emulate that unknowable thing.

Do you remember your first exposure to Lovecraft or the pulps? I was buying all this stuff at the used bookstores in Berkeley as a kid. I don't recall which specific story I read first, but I've always been

a big anthology nut. So I'm sure I'd picked up some anthology somewhere which had a Lovecraft story, and then probably there was an introduction that referenced *Weird Tales*, and then suddenly I was buying every anthology I could get my hands on that included stories from *Weird Tales*.

There was — oh, maybe a couple-year period where it felt like almost every day I discovered some new (to me) writer who was writing at that time. It probably started with Robert E. Howard because I was really into Conan, and he was in *Weird Tales*, and then you pick up *Weird Tales* and you discover Lovecraft and Clark Ashton Smith and all these other guys.

Do you still have all of your books from that time? I have a lot of them, and in many cases, I've tracked down copies where I don't have my originals. In fact, I just went back to Berkeley this past weekend. I hadn't been there in years, but I went back just to look at those used bookstores again and say, "That's where I got my copy of this" and "That's where I got my copy of that." Because it really was the stuff that changed my life.

It was very strange. Some of them had disappeared, but they'd come back. Or some of them used to be on one street and I'd find them on another. And of course some of them were radically different. But one bookstore in particular, Moe's, which is on Telegraph Avenue, was exactly the same. I hadn't been there in 15 years, but I went to particular shelves and probably some of the same books were there. Their folklore section was exactly where it used to be. Their rare book section has the books on the exact same shelves. The supernatural section is exactly where it was. It was a little bit like walking back in time.

So how did the character of Hellboy actually come about? I've heard you say he was based on your father, but where did he come from? Well, I knew the kinds of stories I wanted to do. Coming from ten

DARK HORSE COMICS

HELLBOY II: THE GOLDEN ARMY / DARK HORSE ENTERTAINMENT

gnarled, been-there-done-that kind of guy, which is very much the kind of guy my father is. He's from that WWII generation, and there was something very heroic about those tough old guys. So that's the part of my father that went into Hellboy. Of course, he doesn't talk like my father. He talks like me! But he feels like my father.

Do you have a big interest in World War II? Not really. Not beyond the comic book version of WWII, anyway. That was really important to me when I was reading comics as a kid. I was a Marvel comics guy. And all of my favorite Marvel stuff had at least one foot in WWII. Marvel had all these great WWII villains. They had the Red Skull, they had Baron Zemo . . . they just had these wonderful odd characters. To me, a character like Captain America works better in WWII.

There was just something very heroic and old school about the WWII Marvel stuff. I wanted Hellboy's origin to have one foot in WWII because that just seemed like the real deal, like real comics.

How did you decide to pursue art as a career? I was drawing well before I read *Dracula* — as far back as I could remember. And I don't think I ever found anything else I was even slightly good at. I mean I tried writing a little bit when I was in high school — again, very much inspired by the pulp guys. I tried to come up with this series of fantasy stories with a Conan kind of character. But I just couldn't do it. It didn't click the way drawing did. So I never considered writing as a career. Comics was always something to break into with drawing.

Hellboy used to be small scale and now he's an icon, or approaching one. Has the way that people perceive him now changed your approach? Well, I still think of him as I always have. One of the

years of working for Marvel, I knew I wanted to do supernatural stories and I knew I wanted to do an occult detective kind of a character. I had no interest in creating the kind of character Hellboy really turned into, really. I just wanted a vehicle to do little supernatural stories.

My first instinct was to create a regular human occult detective, like some of the guys I had read about in other people's stories, but I knew I'd get bored drawing a regular person. So I created this monster character just because he'd be fun to draw. But I never intended to get into what that character was. Because I wasn't an experienced writer, the only way I knew how to write a character was to ask: "What would I do, what would I say?"

I wanted a guy who was tough. And kind of older and leathery. I didn't want a snappy wisecracking guy, I wanted a tough,

things that has changed is that it's a lot scarier to sit down and do the comic now that people know about it. It's much easier to do stuff when your motivation is "Nobody expects anything from me, but I'm going to show them something cool." Now, there's a certain level of expectation and that makes it a little bit tougher.

One thing I'm very happy about, though, is that I've stuck to what I wanted that character to be. I could make that comic a much more commercial comic. But even before I did the first movie, I knew the direction I wanted that character to go in. There's a finite Hellboy story. I could have just said, well, I'm going to dismantle that storyline and turn Hellboy into a regular kind of a comic book character where maybe there's the illusion of change but things don't really change. But once I figured out who this character was, I wanted to tell his story.

So right now, I'm happy that I am going in a particular direction that changes him. He evolves, and turns into something else, and the movie hasn't really changed that. A lot more people have seen Hellboy because of the movie, and that's great. But yeah, I'm sticking to what I set out to do.

Are you working on more _Hellboy_ stories right now? I'm writing two _Hellboy_ books right now. I'm writing a 3-issue story for comics legend Richard Corbin based on Appalachian folk tales. It's a story I've wanted to do for a long time, so it's a blast. And then there's the regular ongoing _Hellboy_ storyline. The 8-issue series I'm writing right now takes Hellboy right into the middle of both his life and a big gigantic story arc that really changes him forever.

Duncan Fegredo does the art now, right? I keep telling Duncan that nobody's going to want me back on the book now that they've seen what he can do. He's just great, and I'm really happy with what he's doing. He frees up my writing because there are so many things that he can do so well and so much

better than me. A lot of things I'd thought of in the past would make me go, "Yeah, that sounds great, but I sure as hell don't want to draw it" or "I wouldn't know _how_ to draw that." But Duncan can draw anything.

I don't feel any of the story limitations I felt when I was drawing it myself.

I never would have guessed you felt limited, because you make it look so effortless! Of course, that's the trick, isn't it? Making it look effortless. Yeah, well, it isn't! [_Laughs._] The story I'm doing right now is so huge, there's no way I would have ever approached this thing if I'd thought, wow, I have to draw all this. I probably could have done it, but that would have meant I wouldn't be able to do anything else. As I'm getting older, there are two or three other things I'd like to do. And I had to make the decision: do I do just _Hellboy_ and do it all myself, and know that nothing else will ever get done, or do I say, "Okay, I've done _Hellboy_ myself for 15 years and now I'd like to go on and do some different things."

It was never a question of stopping _Hellboy_. Not just for financial reasons, but because I'm in the middle of a story and I do want to finish it. But the decision not to draw the book was one of the toughest decisions I've ever had to make. And finding someone else to do the book was just . . . not easy.

Did you find Duncan yourself? It never occurred to me that Duncan would be available. I'd been a fan of his for a very long time, but I'd always assumed that Duncan was under contract to DC. So I found this other artist who was really good and really wanted to do it, and he actually drew the first issue of _Darkness Calls_, but it just didn't work out.

So here we were, an entire year behind schedule (we'd actually delayed the book to get this other artist), and we had this issue drawn that we had to throw out. We had to start all over. I was kind of in a panic. And a friend said, "Well, you should try Duncan Fegredo," and I said "Yeah, he's probably not available, but it wouldn't hurt to ask." As it turned out, Duncan actually dropped another project that he was about to start on to jump on the *Hellboy* stuff.

And it worked out! That was a good day. [*Laughs.*]

So now you've written and you've drawn and you've worked in movies. What's your favorite? The more I do stuff other than comics, the more I love doing comics. All the other stuff I've done is more like an interesting side job. I've never done anything else where I thought, "Yeah, maybe I want to do that for a living."

I'll admit I entertained throwing in the towel with drawing, because I get frustrated with my own artwork. You probably know what that's like — there are days when I swear that I'm never going to draw again. "I'm just going to write," I'll say to myself. "It'll make my life so much easier." And sure, I've been doing mostly that for the last couple years. But I'm so keyed up to draw again. I've been doing covers, but I'm really itching to go back and draw comics.

I was watching a clip of you at the con in Birmingham, and you mentioned you were doing more weird personal stories in lieu of *Hellboy* art. Any hints about these? A few years back I did a comic called *The Amazing Screw-On Head*. I think it's one of the two best things I've ever done. It wasn't intended to be commercial, and I didn't know if anyone would like it. It was just for me. As it turned out, people really did like it. So I decided that I want to do more stuff like this. It's what I need to do.

I have a couple of things I've come up with recently that take place in the Hellboy universe — they don't pertain to Hellboy per se, they're just set in that world. But the *Screw-On Head* stuff and stories in that vein are just odd little stories I want to do. I have a collection of them.

Last question. We all know you love monsters. Do you have a favorite monster? If we're talking about movies, it's gotta be Frankenstein. If we're talking about a species of literary creature, it's still gotta be vampires, I think. I never really recovered from *Dracula*. I know how clichéd that is these days. But I'm talking about the old school stuff. No offense to Anne Rice and *Buffy* fans, but it'd be the old, weird shit. That's the stuff I like. ☺

Neil Gaiman's Never Wear

www.NeVerWear.Net

www.NeVerWear.Net

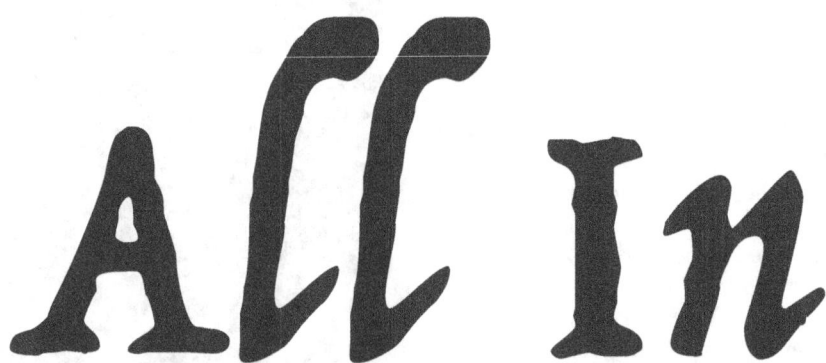

All In

BY PETER ATWOOD

IN WHICH THE
STAKES ARE HIGH
AND THE POT IS
MULTICELLULAR

THE PANEL SLID open with a *shunk*. Two eyes peered out.

"Diagnosis?" the voice asked.

I could smell the cigarette smoke, thick behind the closed door. I nodded.

"Show me," said the voice.

I pulled the creased papers from my shirt pocket, unfolded them against my chest with my free hand, and held them out so the St. Jerome's Infirmary logo was clearly visible at the top. The eyes took in the sealed ice-cream tub hanging from my left hand, then studied the top sheet of the stapled pages long enough to read it twice. The panel shut. I counted my heartbeats as I waited in the dim corridor. The locks on the other side turned. The door creaked open wide enough for me to slip through.

Inside, four players sat around a low wooden table, its veneer cracked and yellow. A matching cloud of yellow cigarette smoke ghosted the visored lamp above.

The eyes behind the door, it turned out, belonged to a gaunt face that fronted a bald head on a tall, gangly frame. He now sat at a tiny metal desk against the wall and extended a hand to take my paperwork. Under the desk was a row of cold boxes: two vacuum cases with handles, two silver insulated containers, and a large, wide-mouthed thermos. Beside them, a small butcher's scale.

Baldy laid the papers on his desk and lifted his chin towards my tub. "Anything in there?"

From the center of the room, I heard the riffle of cards. I shook my head.

Baldy looked at me with surprise.

"It's empty," I said, handing him the tub. A white vapor stream from the dry-ice inside escaped through a crack in the lid and slid down the side like an evaporating snake.

Baldy set the tub under the desk with the other containers, then flipped to the last page of my stapled paperwork. "Everyone here is lung cancer," he commented.

I shrugged.

He examined the signature above my doctor's typed name, his double-jointed finger pressing the paper to the desk. Satisfied, he asked me how much.

"You tell me," I said. I stretched my hands out, palms up. He examined my right hand closely, then pushed my sleeves up to my elbows.

"Hmmph," he said, and counted out twenty-three round, white chips from a tray. I took them in two short stacks, and he waved me to the table.

At the back of the room, a man in a wrinkled tan suit was signing a clipboard held out by a man in green cottons. They stood by a door with a small square window. Tan Suit handed back the pen and watched me. His jacket hung from his shoulders, limp with misery. A green tie was stuffed halfway into its pocket. He looked as if he had some shame to hide, but was too curious to turn away. His eyes stayed on me until I reached the table, scraped back an empty chair, and sat.

I coughed. "Hello."

In response, a card slid towards me. A second slid past to the player on my left. The dealer continued in silence until a pair of cards lay facedown in front of each of us. The four others all anted up with a clatter of chips, and I added mine.

It was two weeks since my doctor had recited my diagnosis to me, my feet dangling in their socks as I listened from his paper-lined exam table. It was sadly common. You hit a certain age and everyone knows someone with an expiry date. Two months, two years — two weeks. But the shock of looking into your doctor's pale brown eyes, your senses numb, as he delivers death's personal ETA — you sweat, your stomach hollows out.

The cool hospital air brushed my ankles. I took a breath. "So what happens next?" I asked him.

It's like being let into a club. The chemical acronyms, the therapy nicknames, the test-result shorthands. And after, all these passwords open new corridors of conversation. "My blood work is up." "My husband's serum count is down." "They bumped my sister to category 4B." Therapy-group comfort offered over coffee.

It only took a few days before I heard the stories. "Mary's father gave his leg for his wife. Well, from the knee down. She's past remission now. Fully healed." The medical profession doesn't talk about the Treatment. It came from Argentina, but the scientist was from Mumbai — or the other way round. The incubation was developed in Korea. A virid is populated, distilled, and injected. It can take two or three tries, but success is eighty-plus percent. It's the donation that's problematic. The virid incubates in living flesh and marrow, enough to make the whole process unethical. Donors must be genetically distant.

I looked at the player to my left. He was a mountain of a man in a short-sleeved, avocado-print shirt. He stretched forward to stub his butt out against the table. His fat arm jiggled. The pile of chips in front of him would easily last till morning. He inspected his cards and dropped them to the table. His cigarette pack lay on the table beside his cards, and after shaking out a fresh white smoke, he slid the carton in my direction.

"No thanks," I said. "I'm leukemia."

"Well, if that don't beat shit," he said, and cupped his lighter to the cigarette between his lips.

The others looked at me. To the left of Fatso was a bearded, narrow-eyed man in his fifties. Vertical wrinkles creased the middle of his forehead. Beside him a player hid behind eighties' Ray-Bans as if this were some Vegas casino. No one was here for the thrill. We rotting players imagine we keep our desperation close to our chest, but all we do is parcel out despair in round pieces of plastic. On my right sat a hunched, gray-haired lady, so thin, shadows cast in the hollow of her collarbone. She coughed and sucked on a cigarette.

This was a lung-patient game — they're the only ones who don't care about smoking. I was here 'cause I needed a new table, desperately. My luck had been bad all week. I lifted the corner of my two cards: diamonds, a jack and queen.

When the betting came around to me, I called, and tossed my one chip in. Fatso beside me did the same. Mr. Beard was dealing this hand. He picked up the deck and peeled off three cards, laying them out face-up. Two low spades and the nine of diamonds. The betting went around again noncommittally. I managed to stay in with only one more chip at risk.

Mr. Beard pulled off another card and turned it up. Eight of diamonds. My stomach did a leap.

Ray-Bans reached forward with a pair of chips, and said, "Two."

The lady to my right tossed her cards forward. "I fold," she wheezed, then pounded a fist against her chest until she hacked out a long cough.

I resisted the urge to check my cards again. I counted four chips from my pile and tossed them forward. "Raise."

"Leukemia Boy is here to play," Fatso deadpanned. The two others still in grunted.

I kept my expression relaxed, and stared at my two cards, still facedown before me. If the final card came up diamonds, I was sitting on a flush. A ten, and I was holding the miracle of a straight flush.

Fatso turned up the corners of his cards, then considered my sixteen remaining chips as if there were some math involved he hadn't encountered before.

"You in?" Ray-Bans asked him finally.

"Well of course I'm fucking in. I'm one treatment from getting clear and clean, so I'm not leaving here without my pound of flesh."

A heavy thunk and a sharp yell came from beyond the square-windowed door. I looked around. Tan Suit and Clipboard were gone.

Fatso laughed. "Sounds like my first eight ounces are being prepared."

For a moment, we all sat listening to the quiet whimpering coming from the next room.

"Just place your bet," Ray-Bans said.

"I'm gonna raise us all another six." Fatso separated out six chips with his chubby index finger and slid them into the pot.

Mr. Beard folded, but Ray-Bans stayed in.

I considered the pile in the center of the table. I turned in my chair and looked back at my tub, leaking CO_2 under the desk. It was empty, a scary thought. If anyone had been paying attention when I came in, they would know. I had the unsettling impression Fatso would take special delight in the fact that I was wearing all my collateral on my bones. The thing is, when leukemia strikes late in life, it's swift. How much time did I have left? Your doctor sees your lips tremble, and his eyes soften. He stresses that it's not precise. Could be more, could be less. Some people live . . . who knows? But all you remember is that first hard and fast date. Mine was up tomorrow.

I pushed my remaining chips into the pot. "I'm all in," I said.

The dealer picked up the deck and lifted the top card. He paused to note it for himself before laying it down. It was the four of clubs.

My teeth clenched. I had nothing! Not even a pair. Not even, not even . . . shit!

"Well, that's a kick in the sweet bits," Fatso chuckled.

I stared at the chips in the pot, going from one to another trying to count the twenty-three specific chips that were mine.

The back door opened and Clipboard escorted Tan Suit back through the room. We all watched. His steps were unsteady. His suit jacket was draped over his left arm, supported in a sling, and at the end of his arm, a round bundle of white gauze was growing a red stain. Clipboard helped him out the door with the locks and then closed it behind. The sound of the latch brought us back to the table.

"I'm out," said Ray-Bans.

I looked at Fatso. His high forehead was greasy; his eyebrows overhung his bloodshot eyes.

"You're all in, aren't you?" he stated.

I ignored him. I needed to see his cards right then. I had to know. "What have you got? Show us what you got."

He shrugged, leaned back with a hand behind his ear, and stretched the other forward to flip over his cards. I stared at them. I looked at mine, and then looked back, disbelieving.

A two of diamonds and a jack of spades. Fatso had nothing!

"Jack high," he said.

"Ha!" I burst out. I leaned forward, my ass lifting right off the chair, and flipped my two precious, wonderful, sweet little cards over. The last one to show was the queen of diamonds. Her Mona Lisa lips smiling serenely for everyone to see.

"Queen high!" I said. "I won. I've got queen high!" I immediately gathered the pot with both hands, scraping the chips towards me. I was laughing out loud and couldn't stop. "I'm cashing out," I declared.

They all looked at me as if I was stupid. The pot was nothing substantial—just a modest beginning to a promising night. But for me, it represented a big enough chunk to get my first treatment incubating. Like I said, luck had been turning on me all week. I wasn't going to risk losing this pot, or anything else, again.

I carried my chips to the desk, grinning. Clipboard was standing beside Baldy, going over papers. "Cashing out?" Baldy asked.

I nodded and handed him my winnings. He returned them to his tray, counting carefully. Clipboard retrieved my ice-cream tub and one of the insulated containers from under the desk and placed them on the floor, the scale between.

"He gets eleven ounces," Baldy announced.

"Eleven," Clipboard repeated, pulling a pair of latex gloves from his green cotton pants and stretching them over his fingers with a snap. A cloudy bath of dry ice overflowed the lip of my tub when he lifted the lid. He packed the CO_2 to the sides, making a pocket inside. Then he unzipped the insulation on the larger container and unclasped the lid, releasing a gasp of pressurized air. Someone shuffled cards back at the table, and Fatso laughed. Clipboard reached inside the container and clattered a handful of bluish-pink digits onto the metal pan of the scale. Three fingers, a thumb, four toes, and something I couldn't identify—a wrist? — frozen and stubby. Their bloodied ends red like the lipstick stain on a half-consumed cigarette.

"Here, you have to sign this," Baldy said.

I stepped to the desk, and I signed where he showed me, holding the pen carefully. He returned my papers and I slipped them into my pocket. Baldy had finished measuring out my salvation, and held my tub up for me, its lid in place, still leaking CO_2.

"You should fix that crack with something."

"Don't worry," I said, "I'm going right to the clinic with this."

I took it from him, gripping the handle as securely as I could with the two remaining fingers of my right hand. ⓔ

Peter Atwood *is a writer and editor who lives in Ottawa, Canada, where he once grew up and to where he returned after living in Toronto, Seoul, and Cairo.*

How I Got Here

BY RAMSEY SHEHADEH

ILLUSTRATION BY STEVEN ARCHER

IN WHICH ANGELIC
SHAPES AND
DEMONIC INTENT
ARE ALL MUDDLED

IT'S JULY, MIDDLE of the afternoon, hot as hell. Henry the Bagman is coming around the corner stuffing his shirt in his pants with one hand and shifting his satchel around on his shoulder with the other. I've got one gun on him and Pedro up in the window over Maxim's has another and Xinhao on the roof across the street has the third. The way it's supposed to work: Henry gets to Father Mancini's front door, he rings the doorbell, the door opens, and then we plug him, all of us at the same time, just rip him to fucking pieces right there on the stoop: Pedro and Xinhao from up high, me up close and personal. We don't so much as graze Mancini. We spatter him with bits of Henry, but we don't hurt him.

It's a message, I guess: my boss, Teddy Dandelion, saying something to Mancini. I don't know what. Guys like Dandelion and Mancini, they talk to each other on a different level than the rest of us. It's all who gets hit and who doesn't, what bits of territory you claim and which ones you leave alone, who you fuck and who you fuck over. I don't know the language, but I guess I *am* the language. Or part of it.

Anyway, Teddy needed his best shooters, people who know how to stay calm and do the job and walk away. That's me, and that's Pedro, but it's *not* Xinhao. Xinhao is a solid gun, and he's loyal as a dog, but he's out of his fucking mind. I did a bank job with him once, easy in and out at this little regional branch over in Virginia. It went smooth: everyone got down on their faces when we told them to, tellers gave up the cash nice and quick, no one tried to be a hero. We were on our way out when Xinhao stopped and turned around and went to the head of the line and just stood there, staring at one of the tellers until he said yes sir and Xinhao said are you ready for me and the teller looked at him and then he looked at me and then he said yes in this really small voice. So Xinhao went up to the counter and said I'd like to make a withdrawal and wrote out a check and slid it through the grating and the teller said sir we don't have any more money and Xinhao shot him in the face. Everyone started screaming. Xinhao turned around and screamed back at them until they settled down. And then he went over to the next teller, a scared blonde surfer-dude-looking guy and did the same thing, spattering the inside of his head all over the sailboat calendar behind him. This time no one screamed, but there were a bunch of people crying now. He went over to the next teller, this kid who looked like she just got out of high school, and started writing out another check.

I don't like people dying when it's not necessary, or at least profitable, so I put a hand on his shoulder and said let's go man. Xinhao turned around and gave me this look. I can see it now. It still keeps me up at night. His face is calm, he's smiling, but there's something going on with his eyes — his pupils keep warping out and in, out and in, like they're breathing, and there's something dark happening behind the whites, shadowshapes skittering like insects, doing

shit I can't make out. No, that's not right. I can make it out. I don't want to. Because some old buried instinct is telling me that if I do figure out what it is I'm looking at I'm going to have to claw my eyes out.

What I wanted to do right then was run. The only thing that made sense was me turning around and running until I collapsed or fell off the edge of something. But I didn't. I said: Come on, man. We got what we wanted. But I said it in a scared little girl voice, and I think that's what saved me, what saved everyone in that fucking bank. Because Xinhao just started laughing; shaking his head and laughing. He put a hand on my shoulder and said: You funny man, Frank. You make laugh. And then he walked out.

These are the people I have to work with.

I'm leaning against a bus shelter, just down the street from Mancini's place, across from a couple of whores flashing their tits at a car full of college kids. I'm wearing a big bomber jacket, so I'm sweating puddles — because you can't hide a sawed-off under a t-shirt. That's one of Teddy Dandelion's maxims. He's got a million of them. Dead men don't talk, but you oughta cut out their tongues anyway, just in case. You can't shoot your best friend, but you can shoot his brother. Women are better than money, but you can't buy money with women. He'll usually pull one out when you're talking to him, then nod and look all serious, like he's just said something worth hearing.

Henry the Bagman's walking up the stairs now. I look at my feet, count the cracks in the sidewalk, listen to the whores cooing their gutter routine. I don't have anything against Henry. He's a good guy. I'll plug him, I'm not saying I won't plug him. But it'll probably keep me up tonight.

My phone rings. I pull it out of my pocket, flip it open.

Back off, says the voice on the other end: Dandelion.

What?

Back off. You're done.

Henry's clear?

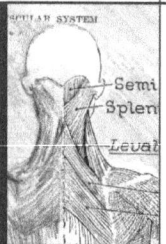

Did I say that? I said back the fuck off. Xinhao's got it.

I look up at the roof across the street. Xinhao's not there. When I look back down he's coming out the front door, hands in his pockets, that little tattoo smile on his face.

You sure, Mr Dandelion?

How many times I got to say the same goddam thing? Turn around. Walk the fuck away.

I flip the phone shut. Xinhao crosses the street, taking it easy, not hurrying, that little tattoo smile on his face. Pedro's not in the window over Maxim's anymore.

I flash back to the bank job, and then I just know: Xinhao's going to do Henry, and then he's going to do Mancini, and then he's going to step over their bodies and go in the house and do the rest of Mancini's family. Mancini's got two little girls, and a boy. The boy's seven, I think. My son's eight.

This is none of my business.

I start running toward Mancini's house.

Henry rings the doorbell.

Xinhao steps up on the sidewalk.

The door opens. Mancini comes out.

Xinhao gets to the bottom of the steps and pulls out a knife.

I slow down, staring at that knife. There's nothing right about it. It's huge, a giant meat cleaver thing, way more knife than you need to kill anything smaller than a elephant. And then it's black, pitch black, like it's made out of tar. But most of all it's just *wrong*, and the wrongness spreads out from it in rings. You can't see it, but you can tell how far it's got by the way people around it act. A lady on the other side of the street drops her groceries and turns all the way around, hands out, palms up, like she's fending off wolves. A baby up the road starts screaming. A dude in a muscle shirt yelps and runs the other way, flat out. Dogs are howling up one side of the block down the other.

Mancini sees Xinhao first. He shouts something, steps back, and Henry spins around, hand already going inside his jacket. Street instincts, but they don't do

him any good, because Xinhao takes two quick steps and pulls his arm back and buries the knife in Henry's chest, all the way down to the hilt. I see the tip of it poke out of Henry's back, and then it's out again, and back in, out and in, out and in. He stabs him five times, arm pumping piston-fast, so quick that the strokes blur together. It's all over before Henry gets his shit together enough to scream.

I'm running full tilt, and I'm almost there when Henry falls against Xinhao, lips peeled back. Blood's leaking out of the cracks between his teeth. Xinhao gets him in a bear hug.

I was expecting Mancini to go inside, call in some heat, grab a gun, come out blazing. But he doesn't do any of that. He says: You can't have him, demon.

Already got him, says Xinhao, laughing. Your boy dogmeat.

I'm at the bottom of the stairs now, so I've got a good view. Xinhao's hugging Henry close with one arm, raising the knife up with the other. But here's the thing: either the knife looked smaller from far away, or it just got bigger, because it's long as a sword now, and wide as a two-by-four. Up close, it's more than black. It looks like a knife-shaped hole in the world.

I lunge for Xinhao.

He brings the knife down in a wide arc, buries it in Henry's back. It slices through his body, out the other side.

Into Xinhao's belly.

Out Xinhao's back.

A square of the world around Henry and Xinhao turns dingy brown, warps in, warps out. It's like I'm looking at their reflection in a sheet of tin.

And then everything snaps back to normal and Xinhao and Henry do what dead people are supposed to do: they fall down. I get out of the way; let them stutter down the steps to the sidewalk. They're still stuck together, like two bugs on the same pin; Henry flopped on top of Xinhao, the hilt sticking out of his back. Xinhao lying there.

He's looking at me. He's smiling.

Mancini's coming down the stairs. He brushes past me, grabs the hilt and pulls it free, kicks Henry off. He looks at Henry for a long time. He looks at me. He says: You're Dandelion's, aren't you?

I nod.

You want to work for me?

I don't answer. It's kind of a fucked up question, under the circumstances.

You deaf? Yes or no?

I shrug. No.

Wrong answer, he says, and jams the sword through my throat.

I freeze, try to breathe. But there's no air. Not for me. Not anymore.

I could tell you what dying feels like, but I won't. You don't want to know.

I'M LYING FLAT on my back, staring at the sky. It's grey and sheet-iron solid, more like a ceiling than a sky. The air smells like the inside of an old cardboard box, tastes like an old gym sock. And it's heavier than it should be. It's like I'm breathing mercury.

I sit up. I'm where I was before, in front of Mancini's house, just outside the city. Except it's not Mancini's house. It's like someone took a picture of his house and blew it up to actual size and propped it up in front of a picture of his front steps, between pictures of the buildings on either side, in the middle of a picture of the rest of the neighborhood. Everything's flat. There aren't any shadows, and the light is white and fluorescent and it comes out of nowhere and there's no sound anywhere.

You just gonna sit there?

I look around. Mancini's standing behind me, popping a clip into an AK-47. He's got wings.

I stand up, slow, letting the dizziness burn off. Mancini's wings are huge, big as an eagle's, and they're made out of white feathers. He's naked. His body is smooth and hairless and ripped, and there's a sort of round bumpish thing where his dick is supposed to be. He looks kind of like a Ken doll.

Are you an angel? I say.

No, dipshit, I'm a ferret.

I reach out and touch one of his wings. It feels real, soft as pillow down. Mancini does something fast and complicated with his hands, and I'm on the ground again, but now my head feels like it's gone through a meatgrinder.

Mancini bends down. You touch my wings again, I'll tear your arm off and shove it up your ass. All the way. Clear?

I wait until there's just one of him, then nod. Clear.

Good. Get up. Moloc's probably halfway to hell already.

Who?

Moloc. He looks at my expression, sighs. The chink.

Xinhao?

Yeah.

He's here?

Jesus. Mancini straightens, looks around, says: He's probably heading for Branch Avenue. There's not much time. Stand up.

I stand up. My stomach does a little backflip, and the pain in my head starts banging through a sledgehammer chorus, but I stay on my feet. He hands me another AK-47. It doesn't have a clip in it.

Here's the plan, he says. You distract him. I get Henry.

Plan, I say, still reeling a little.

He nods and turns around and starts walking. I don't want to follow him, so I stand there for a minute, waiting for a better idea to show up. It doesn't.

I have to run to catch up. I say: Where are we going?

Branch Avenue metro.

Why?

To get Henry away from Moloc.

Who's Moloc?

He looks at me, drops into a grade school patter. He's a demon. He wants to take Henry to hell. We don't want Henry to go to hell.

Xinhao's a demon?

Yeah.

And you're an angel.

Yeah.

And we're in heaven?

Does this look like heaven?

I don't know. I hope not.

We turn a corner, and I see a little crowd of people in the distance, bobbing toward us. There's a giant black something behind them.

It's purgatory, says Mancini. It's where you people get sorted out.

Sorted out?

It's where dead people hang out until they move on.

I know about purgatory. My grandmother was a hardcore Catholic. Her house was plastered with church shit, crosses and pictures of Jesus and Mary and that shriveled pope dude. She'd sit me down every Saturday when my mom dropped me off at her place and tell me all the things that would happen to me if I went to hell. She was a sweet old lady, but the shit that came out of her mouth when she was talking about hell made my little ten-year old sack shrivel up till my balls hurt.

I say: OK. So this is where they decide who's good enough to get in heaven?

Yeah, in theory.

What do you mean in theory?

I mean that's the way it's supposed to work.

But it doesn't?

Not for the last couple thousand years, no.

Then how do you get to heaven?

You know the right people.

Who's the right people?

Me, says Mancini, and grabs my shirt and hauls me onto the sidewalk. The little crowd of people are getting closer. There are two rows of them, three to a row, all naked, all wearing collars, all the collars tied to a harness that runs between the rows into the hands of the giant black thing that's driving them. It's got a horse's head and a woman's body and horns running down its arms. It draws up abreast and turns toward us and opens its mouth and a

baby's head rolls out and drops until it comes up against the limit of the tongue it's attached to and bungies around there, upside down. It doesn't have any eyes. It opens its mouth and makes a sound like a cloud of angry locusts attacking a scream. I piss myself.

Mancini puts a hand on my shoulder, says: Back off. He's mine.

The baby's head leers. Its mouth is way too big for its head. Its teeth are made out of eyes filed down to points. It laughs, then rolls itself up the tongue, back into the mouth.

The black thing shakes the reins, and the people start moving. None of them look over at me. They're just trudging, slumped over and listless, baby steps, one foot in front of the other.

I look at Mancini. What the hell was that?

A six-pack.

A what?

The demons like to take their damned down in sixes. They're all about sixes. Mancini steps off the sidewalk. Let's go.

I look over my shoulder. The horse-head thing leans over and bites off one of the six pack's heads. A stream of blood geysers up out of his neck, splattering the side of the building nearby, but the guy doesn't seem to notice. He keeps moving. I piss myself again.

Jesus, said Mancini, wrinkling his nose. Get ahold of yourself. We're almost there.

Am I going to hell?

How the fuck should I know?

You're an angel.

You're a two-bit crook. What's your point?

But I've done bad things. I've killed people.

And?

Doesn't that mean I'm going to hell?

Like I said. It's not about bad or good. It's about who gets to you first.

We turn another corner and I see the metro's squared-off brown monolith. There's a flash off to my right, and this lady drops out of nowhere. She wearing a patterned

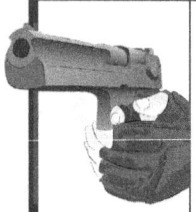

print nightgown, and she's old. She gets up on her feet, looks over at us. I stop.

Keep moving, says Mancini.

Where'd she come from?

I don't know. It doesn't matter. She's dead now.

Is that big horse thing going to get her?

Probably, yeah. But maybe not.

Shouldn't we help her?

Can't help everyone. He grabs my arm and hauls me away.

We get to the metro, hop on the down escalator. Mancini reaches behind his back and pulls out a handful of clips, hands them to me.

These will piss him off, he says. They might even hurt him. But they won't stop him. Remember that. You have to get him to come after you. It shouldn't be hard. He's got a temper like you wouldn't believe. If we're lucky, he'll forget about Henry.

Why can't you do it? I'll grab Henry.

It's against the rules. Me and Moloc, we can't hurt each other.

Why not?

He shrugs. Like I said. It's the rules.

Bullshit.

Just be ready.

What happens if he catches me?

Mancini ignores that, steps off the escalator. The tunnel into the metro is on the dark side of dim, lit by recessed lights in narrow-grated canals on either side of the walkway. The turnstiles at the other end are open. The air down here smells different — somewhere between burnt matches and gunpowder.

Ok, says Mancini. We —

He stops, cocks his head, and then I hear it too: a sort of whining whooshing rushing noise, coming from the inside of the station.

Shit, says Mancini. Come on. He spreads his wings. They're even bigger than they looked folded, nearly twice as wide as he is tall. He jumps, flaps once and flies through the tunnel, takes a sharp left, sails over the turnstiles.

I look behind me, up the escalators, at the hard white light, the quiet, the looking-glass two-dimensional world full of demons and six packs and fuck knows what else. And then I slot in one of my clips and run down the tunnel, through the turnstiles, onto the platform.

The train's blurring into the station. Xinhao's on the edge of the platform. He's got one hand on Henry, who's just sort of standing there, slumped, swaying, staring out at nothing, like he's just smoked a garbage bag of weed. Xinhao's got his back turned to me and he's looking up at the ceiling, a concrete archway honeycombed with recessed squares. He's laughing, shouting stuff in a sort of heavy-metal insect language. Mancini is so bright now he's hard to look at, flying along the curve of the ceiling like a sunrise. I flip off the safety and get down in a crouch, just like they taught me in basic, move up. I'm going too fast to stay totally quiet, but the train should be loud enough to hide whatever noise I'm making.

It isn't, though.

Xinhao turns around, taking his time. He looks exactly the same as he did in the real world, except for one thing: his face is a bunch of different strips of skin quilted together: black and pink and tanned and brown, old and young, lined and smooth. His mouth is made out of at least five different kinds of lips. One of his eyebrows is black and bushy, the other thin, blonde, plucked. It's not a Frankenstein job: everything fits together fine, like a jigsaw puzzle.

Hello Frank, he says. He's smiling. How the kids?

His eyes don't match. I can see that now. One of them is green, the other brown.

I look over at Henry. He's missing an eye.

That sets me off. I don't know why. I prop the butt against the crease of my shoulder and start shooting.

Xinhao takes it full in the chest, lets go of Henry, staggers back, glances off the incoming train. I follow him, keeping my finger on the trigger until the gun's clicking over empties. Out of the corner of my eye, I see Mancini streak past.

Xinhao sees it too. He tries to get up. I slot in another clip, aim, fire. He goes down.

The train doors slide open. I glance over. The car's full of stoners, all of them just standing there, staring straight ahead, like tranquilized cattle.

I pop in my last clip. Xinhao's getting up. He doesn't look hurt, and he's not smiling. Xinhao's creepy when he's smiling, but it turns out he's absolutely fucking terrifying when he's not.

Mancini and Henry are gone. I don't turn around to check, but I know. It's just me, and Xinhao, and a trainful of stoned dead damned people.

A chime sounds, and a smooth voice says: Doors closing. Please step away from the doors.

I bring the AK up and fire, catching Xinhao in the head. He staggers, drops down to one knee. I take two steps back, into the train, firing still, hoping my ammo outlasts the doors.

It does. Another chime, and the doors slide shut. The train starts moving.

I watch Xinhao through the window. He crouches and springs and flattens himself against the glass, hands splayed frogstyle, then jacks his head back and slams it into the window. It shudders and cracks. He tips his head back again, smashes the glass, and now the crack's a cobweb, spreading out toward the corners. He tips his head back again. I put the barrel of the gun up against the middle of the cobweb, and pull the trigger right as he's coming if for another one. I'm shooting dregs now. The last of my ammo blasts out into his forehead, snaps his head back, then blows him off the train.

We go into the tunnel.

I stand there for a minute, breathing the panic out of my body. The train's moving fast, and the wind blowing in through the hole in the window is deafening. I turn to the nearest dead guy. A big fat guy with a giant bushy beard, hair in a pony tail.

I say: How's it going?

He doesn't answer. I wave a hand in front of his face, flick his earlobe. Nothing. Just standing and swaying and staring, in his own little world. Not all that different from regular, alive subway people, really, except for the being dead.

The train puts on the brakes, starts slowing down. Next station coming up fast, and fuck knows what's waiting for me there. I check my magazine. Empty. I close my eyes and say a prayer to whatever god is running this fucking show.

That's when it hits me.

Branch Avenue is the last station on the green line.

This train shouldn't be going anywhere. It should be turning around and going the other way.

I push my way up to the head of the car, look through the door into the next one.

It takes me a while to see it. There's something making its way down the car, a sort of distortion, like the shimmer that comes off hot tarmac. Whenever it touches one of the stoners, they go nuts: they're flailing and screaming and ripping at themselves, at each other.

I turn around and run the other way, pushing stoners out of the way. I get to the opposite door, open it, step through into the next car. There's three cars between me and the back of the train. I look over my shoulder. The distortion is coming fast, and stoners are going apeshit not ten feet away. The sound of their screaming drills into my head.

Two more cars.

One.

I'm at the end of the last car when it touches me. I don't know how to explain what it feels like. Imagine the worst pain you've ever had, then triple it and live inside of it for a billion years. Then imagine feeling that same pain through your children for a billion more. That's a start.

I slam through the last door, off the

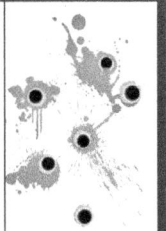

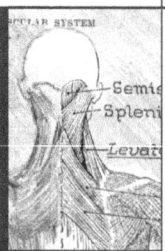

train, onto the tracks. Every fuse in my brain is blown, but I manage to get on my feet and stagger back up the tunnel. I go maybe a hundred feet, then look back.

All the stoners inside the train are writhing like downed powerlines now, throwing themselves at the windows, tearing off their clothes, and then their skin. I don't blame them. I got a little taste of what they're feeling right now. I wouldn't want my body anymore either.

I turn back up the tunnel and start walking, trying not to hear the screams.

MANCINI'S WAITING AT the top of the escalators. You made it, he says.

I drop down on my ass, lean up against the side of the brown monolith, say: Fuck you.

Fuck you too. Henry's on his way to heaven, if it's any consolation.

It is, but I don't want him to know that. I say: Can I go home now?

Home?

Yeah.

No home for you, my friend. You're done with that place.

I knew that already, on some level. I think about my boy, my wife. If my dad hadn't beat the shit out of me every time I cried when I was a kid, I'd cry now.

OK, fine. What do I do now?

That's why I'm here. You get to work for me.

I work for Teddy Dandelion.

You know what Teddy Dandelion is?

Yeah. He runs Ward 8. He gives me money to do bad things.

One, that don't mean shit down here. Two, his real name is Abaddon. He also goes by Angel of the Abyss and The Destroyer. Right? So you may want to consider a lateral move here.

What's the difference? You said it yourself. The only thing that matters is who gets to you first.

Right. But it matters a *lot*.

He steps aside, and I see the old lady from earlier, the one that dropped out of the flash in the sky. She's as stoned as the rest of them.

I look at Mancini. And?

And you get to escort this nice old lady to heaven. If you do a good job, maybe you'll get other jobs.

Why the hell would I want more jobs from you?

This is me offering to help, Kinsley. It won't happen again.

I close my eyes, open them, stand up, say: I lost my gun.

Mancini pulls an Uzi out of I don't know where, hands it to me. Hold on to this one, dipshit.

Where am I going?

National.

Airport?

Yeah. Put her on the first plane you see.

What if I try to get on it too?

It doesn't work that way. You live here now. Get used to it.

He turns around and blows out his wings, flaps them a couple of times, rises a couple feet off the ground. Welcome to the team, dipshit.

And then he flaps his wings again, hard enough to blow me a couple steps back, and takes off into the metal sky.

The city goes quiet.

I check the Uzi's chamber, drop the extra clips in my pocket. I look at the old stoner lady. She kind of reminds me of my grandma. I put my arm around her, and we start moving west, toward heaven. ⊚

Ramsey Shehadeh *is a computer nerd trapped in the body of a computer geek. Under various pseudonyms, he has produced such enduring classics as "Oliver Twist," "Gone With the Wind," and "The Bible." He subsists entirely on absinthe and the blood of his enemies, and his dreams of world domination are often shattered by the indescribably loud howling of his beagle. You can find him online at http://doodleplex.com.*

Belair Plaza

BY ADAM CORBIN FUSCO

ILLUSTRATION BY VICTORIA ALEXANDROVA

IN WHICH WE DISCUSS VARIOUS THINGS THAT, LIKE GUNS, DO NOT KILL PEOPLE

O N A SLIGHT rise overlooking Belair Plaza, behind a Mini Market that has been robbed only twice despite constant patronage by a decidedly sketchy element, is found the body of a teenage girl. We will not describe the condition of the body. Suffice it to say that the body lies in a certain posture cradled by autumn leaves and surrounded, as such places always are, by decades-old cigarette butts, rusted Coke cans, and anonymous shreds of newspaper.

In an analysis of the situation you must take into account the surrounding environment, most especially Belair Plaza. It is a line of shops built when the rest of Gladesboro was built, in the early 1960s, as part of a Levitt town that offered affordable housing in exchange for conformity. In this city of Gladesboro there is a section referred to as Belair, though no sign proclaims it so, and in the northern portion near the golf course there is a Belair Drive. The name Belair is obscure in its origins. It elicits an associative link with an unattainable higher class, though this image is antithetical to the plaza itself. There are countless locales across the country named Belair.

The back of Belair Plaza is a whitewashed, mottled wall of loading platforms which front an access road and a wood. Utility meters stain the wall with rust. Dumpsters ooze a sickly sweet substance. If you look closely at the whitewash you can see, as if at a photographic negative, the remnants of sandblasted graffiti that can be read again, like palimpsests. This is the real graffiti of decades past, not the artistic tagging of names. Here is Boner, Fuck, and Dick. Here is the iconographic phallus composed of two circles connected to a length rounded at the top, identical to the design carved into the lava-block streets of Pompeii pointing to the locations of brothels. You must not dismiss where these inscriptions likewise may point.

The façade of Belair Plaza has never changed despite the efforts of postmodern architects to squat a pyramid shape above the stores of contemporary "strip malls" elsewhere, or offer a village aspect through scrolled signage proclaiming each "shoppe." Here there is a series of planters in front of the stores composed of low brick rectangular walls that, since the plaza is built into a gradual slope progressing upwards left to right, are taller on one side than the other. The planters are irresistible to children to walk upon as if a balance beam, a precarious perch between sidewalk and prickly bushes; but a child walking down the wall soon finds himself too high off the ground to jump. As you walk next to them now they seem too low to bother. The foliage here has not changed. The patterns created by serrated shiny leaves and yellow marigold blooms are the same as if the old plants had never died.

The anchor store, as such things are now called, is a grocery store that has never changed names and belongs to a chain. Walking into it you notice a hint of the same smell you remember from entering the place truly countless times in the past. The cheerful, whistling black man who loaded packages and a prattle of pithy advice into customers' cars is gone, but this store still exudes its haven-like atmosphere. This is the "safest" store of all in the plaza. Nothing bad may happen here.

Belair Plaza can be regarded as of two parts divided by the anchor store, which sits a third of the way from the left side. The slope leading to the body of the teenage girl progresses to the right. The stores toward the left possess an empty quality, as if the plaza starts with the grocery store instead. This left side is less substantive, as if the proprietors moving into these spaces already know their businesses are going to fail.

Sitting on the left shoulder of the grocery store is a delicatessen that likewise has not changed its name, but still attains the "left side" aspect because you have never been inside it. It still holds a quality that prevents you from entering. To the left of the deli are two or three small spaces that you cannot remember containing anything of notice, and even now your eye skips over them. Perhaps they had been or are office spaces for lawyers or entrepreneurs. One has neat white lettering on its glass door proclaiming R. H. Cliden & Associates, and looking into the blinds you see bare carpet, white partition walls, a planter, and a chair, until the grey light of the lowering sky washes out the image.

Next to these squats the expanse of the Good Hearts Thrift Store. People donate furniture here for tax deductions. The sullen interior is shrouded behind the glass. Black women in paisley scarves and white women with smoke-leathered faces pick over tables piled high with cardboard-backed packages of generic pantyhose, shriveled bras, meloncolored throw rugs, and the snapping gold clasps of matte-black pocketbooks. The floor is the same tile used in your elementary school but shellacked with a thicker layer of dust. The smell is of old books; the lighting is that of attics. The furniture for sale here is anonymous, constructed of unclassifiable wood that entraps the ghosts of musty clothes. The gargoyle-smiles of tarnished brass pulls reflect the ones made by the light poles in the parking lot with their double

arcs, a leering grin with anomalous linkages to the grimace of George Corley Wallace's would-be assassin as he is led away from a crowd, witnessed by you on television after school long ago — a sudden crack of gunfire that took place, it so happens, in a neighboring town.

This store makes your suspect list. This furniture has witnessed countless ejaculations in rooms smelling of Lysol.

The leftmost occupant of the plaza — separated from the rest by a space that flickers between a paint store and a lawn care center — sells trophies and plaques. It is confusing to you how such a place could stay in business. How many people win trophies?

How many people need brass plaques? But they sell ice skates and cheerleader accessories as well, and it becomes clearer. The patrons of such a store have daughters that possess the kind of pure, bright-eyed excitement found only at a certain age and nowhere else in the universe. (This becomes more significant when we get to Scanlin & Sons Dry Cleaners.) The innocence associated with state finals, pom-poms on skates, cheerleader batons, laces, white leather, and waterproofing cream indicates the need for this establishment to sit at the end of the plaza away from other influences.

The trophy store goes on your suspect list.

To the immediate right of the anchor store is a pizza parlor. It has changed names through the years — Maria's, Assisi's, Roma Delight — but never its decor or nature. The tables are covered with red-and-white checked tablecloths upon which squat glass shakers of Parmesan cheese and red pepper flake. Wood paneling hides moldy plaster. One must stand at the counter for a long time before getting service even if the place is empty, which it usually is, but the pizza is good and made with care. The jukebox plays only puppy love songs that teach love as loss. The wanness of these songs is periodically drowned out by the beeping of a Pong game and an Indy 500 pinball machine.

Next to this is a store that changes proprietorship so rapidly that the sign on the façade displays bare fluorescent tubes. It is a knick-knack kind of place. In significant times it was a macramé store. Though we refuse to describe the condition of the body, this binding referent must not be dismissed.

At this point we come to Scanlin & Sons Dry Cleaners. On the wood-paneled front desk is affixed an Edwardian "R." Scoop plastic chairs of aqua blue recall a 1950s vision of progress. On the wall perches a clock radiating wooden sunrays. Nothing changes here, most especially Mr. Scanlin himself. The "sons" have never been in evidence. Like the flickering shutter of old-timey film, a progression of young girls has worked the counter, always assertive, energetic, knowing, and willing. Scanlin possesses a leering confidence. He talks loudly and moves rapidly. He is cheerful in a neurotic, sweaty way. He is tall, balding, and thin. One can never take his picture; his insatiable appetite creates a nervous energy that blurs film. Perhaps a black-and-white Polaroid — the kind from which you must peel away the sticky facing after a wait of three minutes — taken at Christmas time would show him posed in front of a mantel with his arm around a small shoulder, revealing forced grins; but the faces would still be pasty-white from the flash. If you ever did obtain a proper image, his face would be a grotesquerie of bulging eyes and gritted teeth, as if he were being electrocuted. The grey polyester of his pants hiding a pickled but enormous phallus would be stained black with the afterimage of endless spills of sperm.

Scanlin, a little too obviously, is at the top of your list. Even with boys, his finger lingers a little too long when measuring an inseam.

Next to Scanlin & Sons Dry Cleaners is Belair Liquors, run by a pair of business-like Italian brothers who might be twins. Their sons, or the sons of one, run it now, and are often mistaken for the elders. A dusty blow-up sex doll sits waist-high in a tub of beer cans and holds in its outstretched arms a sign reading "Sale $2.99 6/pack."

Further along is the drugstore, notable for thick mass market paperbacks with embossed covers and huge typefaces, the stocky counter girl with the faint mustache, and outrageous prices.

The white stripe on the barber shop's rotating pole has yellowed. It is unclear whether the barrel-bellied old man with the crew cut and short legs, who pockets bills from the cash register at every ring-up, is visible through the glass. The accounts of boys coming out of this establishment with rashes (cuts) on the backs of their necks are attributed to something that must have happened in their sleep.

You have never known the name of the Chinese restaurant. A tobacco-colored filigree of wood or plastic adorns the windows on the outside. Dragon shapes emerge from this, though they turn abstract if looked at closely. Burgundy drapes hide the interior. It has always been so. There is never an indication whether this place is open or closed. You have never seen the curtains drawn back. You have never seen people entering or leaving. The Chinese restaurant creates a dark spot in Belair Plaza, a blank space. Walking beside it, your steps quicken, and it seems to turn invisible. The fact that the drapes are now open to reveal a quite ordinary restaurant with round tables and recessed lighting is indicative to you of something severely wrong.

Our altitude is increasing rapidly at this point, reaching the outer edge of the plaza. The stores here, as on the leftmost side, are gaining an ethereal quality. The roof over the sidewalk has been leaking. Wet stains coat the cracker-colored squares under your feet. Here is the narrow store with the high steps leading up to it that is the Bippy Center, a community center for teens that sells rolling papers. This is a mecca for bean-bag chairs, where tiny pink-polished nails reach for the gnarled stub of a joint.

The rightmost space may be dismissed. It has never had an identity. It has been some kind of hardware store or paint store or auto parts store or bicycle store, and now the independent video establishment here is doomed, though it may escape extinguishment as long as it does no business.

Across a length of asphalt, which leads to the back of the plaza, is a concrete stairway. At the summit you must cross a street. Directly across the street is a worn path through the woods leading to the back of the Mini Market. Before you get there, you can find the body of the girl.

The stairway is steep. The paint on its bent railing is the color of pool water. Etched into the paint and making it flake with rust are the words Mandy + Brian, Shell + Tommy, Tim + Angela. As you ascend, it is possible to gain a unique prospect of Belair Plaza. You are looking down the length of the entire building. It shrinks as you progress. The yellow lines of the parking lot fade. The roof is covered in gravel, tar, and black plastic sheeting. Smoke lazes out of pipe vents. The bricks of the walls crumble with seepages of calcium.

The cold metal of the rail vibrates. The wind swirls, caught in the pocket between the hill and the building. Your throat constricts. Grit grates under your feet in the form of sand, broken green glass, candy bar wrappers, striped straws, orange french fry containers, stones, pop tops, and chewing-gum foil. These items are disturbed in a pattern indicative of an abrupt scuffling of shoes. It would be difficult to drag someone up these steps, but not impossible. You weep.

Certainly such things do not happen as frequently as they did in the past. You were not kidnapped and then brainwashed. You were not buried alive in a school bus. You were not impaled with a safety pin through the heart. The creeks and ditches webbing the neighborhood no longer hold menace. The frequency of incidents that prompted school officials to paint red bands on the trees bordering the forest at your school, beyond which you were not to walk, have faded with the expansion of growth rings. The school, after all, is now a YMCA.

Places do not kill people. Entropic ennui in a location can be overcome without murder, like letting steam out of a kettle. It smells of cheap aftershave and store-brand laundry detergent, and is practiced with a highly evolved system of behavior disguised as accidental that cannot be proven otherwise. The wrong change is given. Price tags are missing or switched. Bags are not offered. A clerk asks a roundhouse of condescending questions. A box of cookies is found crushed after purchase but wasn't noticed to be in this condition when on the shelf.

It is polyester. It is lipstick on cigarette butts. It is sunshine blasting through a dirty car window.

Places do not kill people, but there may be a pocket of geosynchronous circumstances that create conditions where the steam is cumulative, and erupts.

Speculation is fruitless. Many things have changed since the last time you walked this slope. Many things have not.

There are countless locales across the country named Belair. ℮

Adam Corbin Fusco's *fiction has appeared in* The Year's Best Fantasy and Horror, *vols. 7 and 17;* Science Fiction Age; *and* The Best of Cemetery Dance. *His Web site is www.adamcorbinfusco.com.*

An Invitation Via Email

BY MIKE ALLEN

From: Giles Milko <gjmilko@va.fairleigh.edu>
To: Miranda Statzler
<mastatzler@va.fairleigh.edu>
Subject: Excellent piece in the Critic!
Date: Wed, 5 Nov 2003 11:12:03 -0500
X-Mailer: Internet Mail Service (4.4.1545.48)

Hello, Ms. Statzler, Giles Milko here. Hopefully you remember me from the conversation we had last Thursday at the after-hours faculty party. I have to say I really enjoyed your essay in the newest Fairleigh Critic on the subjective nature of fear. I'm very much in agreement with your contention that the most extreme phobia or paranoia, no matter how crippling, can be overcome through the gradual building up of confidence. I must say that aside from being informative, I found your piece also to be quite entertaining, especially the self-deprecating wit you used in describing your efforts through therapy to overcome your fear of spiders. In my head I could hear the mental squeals of horror as Dr. Sherrill placed the tarantula in your hand; then feel the overwhelming burst of triumph as you set the spider gently on the table and realized: I did it! I did it!

Some of the asides in your article made me realize (Gods, can I be dense sometimes) that when you spoke of concerns about "arcane rites" in response to the invite to my Halloween party the next evening, that you possibly weren't kidding and perhaps had some genuine anxieties. I really should stress that my wife and I had planned for the Halloween party to be occult-free — no spirits other than the liquid sort!

I realize I've gained a facetious reputation among students over the years, usually for little more than addressing poor Giordano Bruno's attempt to understand the world through sorcery in a History of Science class! (I must say though, Bruno did have a knack for concocting ominous-looking magical symbols — it's no wonder the Church made kindling out of him.) Obviously some such rumor reached you long before our first encounter in the flesh — so as soon as I finished your essay I felt compelled to write you and set things to right.

The thaumaturgical ceremonies conducted in my home are not fearful, black-robed affairs reserved for special nights. They're actually very casual things, held Sunday mornings or the occasional Saturday if someone wants to see a football game instead. They're not geared toward any more sinister a purpose than furthering the careers of the participants. (I, for one, need the boost. Consider that I teach nine credits a week, write a column for the town paper and complete a new book every two years. Do you really think I could do all that without "outside" help?)

A few faculty members take part, as well as one freelance writer from town who needs to combat his "day job braindrain." Sometimes writers or artists from out of town make "guest" appearances. It's all quite open and friendly. No one dresses up — T-shirts and sweats, in fact, are perfectly acceptable attire.

Of course, there has to be a sacrifice. Our ideal choice is one of those horribly misguided individuals (sadly, almost always a parent) who goes to the school board wanting to ban this book or that book, or goes whining to town council to cancel Halloween as a Satanic holiday. Unfortunately for the world, but good for us, there seems to be no shortage of them (though we've done our best, I swear). And if we can't get our hands on an adult, one of their children will do the trick — these sorts of genes don't need to spread.

The sacrifice doesn't need to be conscious,

but he or she does need to be alive, so that each of us can take a small bite of their still-beating heart. Making the proper cuts to remove a heart this way is frankly rather tricky, though we've all gotten well-practiced. Of course we have to pass a "chalice" around — a coffee cup will do, really — for that token chaser of blood. Then we summon the "outerdimensional persona" (that's the politically correct term these entities seem to prefer nowadays.) Now at this point you might experience some of that anxiety you discussed in your essay, but there's no need to worry. We've drawn the right symbols and circles so that the persona (our favorite is a fellow with a pleasantly dry wit named Mephisto) can't do anything other than talk. Once we see his (its? Gender is never clear with these things) disembodied head hovering over the remains of the sacrifice, we pepper him with questions about the status of his labors with regard to our projects (in the ears of which editors or agents has he whispered, what bargains has he struck, did he give an appropriate nightmare to the woman who wrote that rude rejection, etc.)

After we get our update, he heads back to New York. Really, that's it. He (it?) takes most of the sacrifice for sustenance until next weekend. We knock on my study door so my wife knows we're done, and she'll usually bring in something like sweet rolls and hot chocolate, so we dig into those while we sit around talking shop. What's left over of the sacrifice we give to the new puppies, who love their weekend meal (it's usually cooked a bit as a result of the persona's presence.) Of course, the cat doesn't want to be left out, but her teeth have gone bad, so she just gets a little saucer of blood.

You're probably wondering why the authorities have never barged in on us. Well, as a condition of this arrangement, Mephisto or whichever persona we happen to dial up erases the memory of the sacrifice from the minds of everyone who ever knew them (except for us.) So if no one remembers their existence, no one misses them. (And we've managed to improve the gene pool a tad in the process.) Of course, if there's a lot of physical evidence left behind, like say, wedding albums or newspaper articles, the

entity will have to work a bit harder to make sure everyone's curiosity is sufficiently dulled. But overall it's a very efficient system.

I'm not sure how close the lot of us has gotten to achieving our ultimate goals, but these weekend get-togethers do seem to help. You're certainly welcome to come by this weekend (or any weekend of your choosing, there's no hurry) and join in. Perhaps we could help you to produce more wonderful essays like the one I just read. Or maybe there are some solidly grounded fears (I hear rumors of a troublesome ex-husband?) that we can help put to rest for good.

I hope all of this helps to reassure you.

Yr obt. servnt.,

Milko

* * *

From: Giles Milko <gjmilko@va.fairleigh.edu>
To: ScienceFaculty@fairleigh.edu,English-Faculty@fairleigh.edu,ligotti@morbid.net
Subject: Apology
Date: Mon, 11 Nov 2003 7:48:03 -0600
X-Mailer: Internet Mail Service (4.4.1545.48)

To all: My sincerest apologies!

Ms. Statzler seemed like an intelligent, inquisitive woman who would understand the benefits of our arrangement. How could I have predicted she would interpret my explanatory email as a joke? I promise to be more careful in screening new members henceforth.

I'm still not precisely a master of this new e-mail system, so if you received this message in error and have not a clue to whom I'm referring — well, just take comfort that things are exactly as they should be. :-)

All best,

Milko ℮

Mike Allen lives in Roanoke, Va. with his wife Anita, a comical dog and a demonic cat. He's the editor of *Clockwork Phoenix* and *Mythic Delirium*. His most recent fiction has appeared at *Helix* and *Cabinet des Fées*.

Mainevermontnewhampshiremass

BY NICK MAMATAS

ILLUSTRATION BY SIMONE VAN DEN BERG

IN WHICH WE ASK
WHY ALL THE
HORROR AUTHORS
SEEM TO LIVE IN
THE SAME PLACE

SAMUEL BEY HAD never seen this before. It was traffic, a midtown Manhattan snarl, but this wasn't 54th and Lex and he hadn't just stumbled out of a gin and steak lunch with his agent McCage and that assistant of his, Kathleen, the one with the breasts that stared at you while you ate. He was in Rover's Corner, the little town in the little state on the border of other little states deep in the gnarled wilds of New England. Rover's Corner was the town Sam Bey had made famous.

Too famous, Sam thought. His books had made Rover's Corner a little bit of a tourist destination ever since *The Dimmening* came out years ago, but pigeon-chested nerds couldn't afford the SUVs and sleek German vehicles currently standing between Sam and the raspberry chocolate frappes at Copley's Dinner and Barber-B-Que. Even today Sam still winced at the thought of his first copy editor, at the smug little Vassar bimbette who thought "Barber-B-Que" was a typo.

Can't a man drink a frappe and get a Johnny Unitas haircut at the same time anymore? Whatever happened to America?

SUVs happened to America. Political correctness. PG-13 movies. Comics that cost more than a dollar. Nick At Night instead of just getting sick from playing in the snow all weekend and getting to stay home on the couch watching *Bewitched* and *Gilligan's Island*. Sam had had a personal assistant and let her go after she didn't get a famous reference to that episode of *I Love Lucy* in which Tennessee Ernie Ford shows up as "Cousin Ernie" after walking across Long Island — it was just impossible to get good help these days. And then there was the whole Internet and those fans and message boards . . .

But enough of these current evils, Bey thought as he finally parked his H3 across three spots outside Copley's. *It's time for the showdown.* There was an ancient darkness awakening in Rover's Corner and it was up to Samuel Bey to stop it. Sam got out of his car and stepped onto the unpaved but consecrated ground. Yes, consecrated with the spirit of goodness and the power of friendship and the memories of old loves and childhood joys and ice cream sandwiches and whoopie pies and sneaking over the border into New Hampshire to buy fireworks and then sneaking over the other border into Vermont just to set them off and and and . . .

And then he began to scream.

"SAMMY!" SOMEONE SHOUTED back. It was Bart Black, all smiles and swirling wisps of cigarette smoke. Bart Black was a horror author too — splatterbop, all jazzy riffs on thrill kills and sex murders. *The Nether Knifepoint* was his magnum opus, if his friend Sammy didn't say so himself. "That was the best vag-stab scene I've ever heard of," Sam had told Bart after Sam's wife had read the manuscript up to that point and then stopped. Sam never read anything he hadn't written himself. Sam's

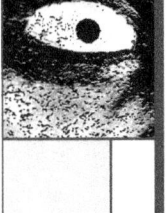

blurb — "It'll get you right in the gut, and then a little bit lower" — was enough for six printings and four movie options (but no movies). Bart owed Sam. Big time. And tonight, he thought, he'd have to pay it back. All of it. "Are you all right?"

"I . . . " Sam started, his voice raspy and weak from the scream. "I don't know why I did that."

"It's been going around," Bart told him. "You'd better come inside. It's filling up fast in there." Bart hiked a thumb back toward Copley's, and then expertly flicked his cigarette butt out of his hand. The sizzling ember spiraled through the night like a drunken lightning bug, then winked out in the darkness beyond the diner.

"Copley's never fills up," Sam said.

"Tonight's no ordinary night."

From inside the diner, someone began to scream.

COPLEY'S WAS ALL filled up. *God*, Sam thought to himself (or he *thought* he thought this only to himself), *this looks like the hotel lobby at Fangula's Freak Con.* And it did, except that this was no lobby, and it certainly wasn't off Exit 12 on the Jersey turnpike. They were all there, not just Bart. Surrounded by a handful of the younger writers, the guys who still sported heavy-metal T-shirts and mullets over balding pates — Sam always imagined that their hairdos were trying to crawl down their backs and escape — was Ophelia Darque, the screamer. Her corset wasn't on too tightly — well, it *was*, but in a good way — she was screaming to show off the fangs and just how widely she could open that lipstick-slathered mouth. The kiddie writers (Sam thought of them as the Kiss Army) laughed and applauded and all but waved their arms and said, "Look at me, Ophelia. Don't look at these guys, look at me!" As a simultaneous circlejerk and collective cockblock, the scene was both Escheresque and Kafkaesque. Sam liked that he had thought of that line, and put it in his mental files to

use in a book sometime. Or twelve times.

Thomas Hittler, a paunchy professor type, waved from across the crowded room. "Hallo, Sam. It's Hittler, back here!" Thomas pronounced it *Heet-tleer*. "The extra T is for extra terror!" Sam had suggested to Thomas once, but Thomas chose to bear his unfortunate surname with a Midwestern stoicism utterly alien to Sam. They were friends, Sam and Thomas, close ones, but Sam never could get over his initial impression of his colleague: Thomas looked like someone had painted a face on an egg and set it on top of a starched collar. Thomas was up and on his feet now, a frappe in each hand, and pushed his way to the door. "Samuel, good to see you," he said and he shifted one of the frappes to the crook of his arm to free up a hand for a meaty one-armed hug. "I think we can begin now."

"Uh . . . " Sam started. "What's going on?"

"Showdown," Bart said.

"Showdown," Thomas said too, with a serious nod.

"Oh man, Samuel Bey!" said some scrawny kid who had materialized right by Sam's left elbow. "Hi, it's me," said the kid, who was actually wearing a tuxedo. "Remember me, from the Lenore Awards banquet, when you won the lifetime achievement award? I wore what I was wearing then in case you came, so you'd remember me."

"You're my biggest fan," Sam said. " . . . Jeremy?" That was a safe guess. Everyone under the age of thirty seemed to be named Jeremy these days.

Jeremy beamed. "You do remember me! I'm so glad I was able to make it. I spent years submitting stories, but finally one got published. Do you read *Dark Somethings*, Mister Bey?" It was a photocopied zine that Sam received in the mail every eighteen months or so. He found that the paper stock was good for rolling joints, so appreciated the free subscription. "I remember back in 1989 you writing in that essay that *Dark Somethings* was the future of h—" Jeremy kept talking, but Sam turned his bad ear toward him.

"What is all this?"

"We should get the meeting underway," Thomas said. "Here's your frappe." He handed Sam the extra glass.

And then someone began to scream.

"YO! YO, YO!" Scrape was on the counter, all denim and mirrorshades. "Wooaaaaaw!" he howled like a brewpub stud doing his best *Houses of the Holy* impression. "Glad you all could make it! We need to get this show on the muthafuckin' rooooaaaaaad!" Scrape was a little too old and a little too famous (and a little too fat, these days) to be Kiss Army, but he sure was annoying. Scrape liked to write about rockstar wendigos and snorting coke out of the quivering genitals of fourteen-year-old hookers. Sam had remembered wondering if that hadn't been Scrape's car a few ahead of his back in the traffic snarl. Scrape had a nice 2002 Chrysler PT Dream Cruiser with the wood paneling, and a DIE YUPPIE SCUM bumper sticker that had been lovingly cared for and transferred onto every new bumper Scrape had owned since 1984.

"We all know why we're here, and we all know who you've come to hear" — Sam stepped forward, not knowing why he was there at all any more, except that the Showdown was imminent and only he knew how to stop evil from overwhelming Rover's Corner and maybe even the whole world. He tried to remember some quick anecdotes about the early days to tell his crew, who seemed to all be horror writers of one stripe or another. "Nigel St. Carnal!" Scrape finished.

Silence. Well, except for the buzzing of the junebugs on the screendoor. They were attracted to the light, hugging the mesh to keep from the darkness outside. Even the insects could sense it. The Showdown.

Nigel rose from his chair in the dark corner of Copley's, and stepped onto it and

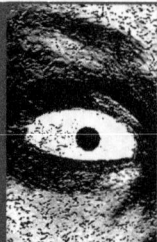

then from there onto the top of a squat cigarette machine of the sort you just don't see in New York City anymore. A pang of nostalgia washed over Sam; he could taste the ash and fire of a good smoke on his tongue, and in his throat. But he couldn't smoke anymore, not since the accident, and the surgeries. The butchers in green and white, cracking open his sternum like a nut . . . Sam gulped down the sensation and his memories, leaving it bitter in his stomach.

"It is heartening that so many of us have come. That so many of us have felt the call from so far away," Nigel said, "to come back here to Rover's Corner. To my hometown."

"Your hometown," Sam said. All heads turned. "Nigel, you're British."

"I'm Welsh," Nigel corrected, gently.

"Be that as it may, this isn't your hometown. I lived here for thirty-two years, my whole life up to the time I had to move down to New York. I didn't even meet you until I was forty, and that was at Fangula!"

"There are many ways to call a town home. The St. Carnals have been a part of this town's history since the land was purchased from the Abenaki. The church in which you were baptized, Sam, was founded by my great-great-great-great grandfather."

"And I went to summer camp here!" said Jeremy.

"Madge's family has a summer place in West Rover's Corner. On the Vermont side. Remember, Sam, I invited you fishing there once?" Thomas said. Sam didn't remember. The 1990s were really a big blur anyway.

Sam looked around, and he met Bart's gaze. Bart shrugged. "I think I bagged a waitress here once." Then he flashed a smile. "I think she thought I was you."

"God," said Sam. He turned on his heel and pointed at Scrape. "How about you, Mister L.A.?"

"I went to Wiggleton Prep!" Scrape said, suddenly defensive, though it wasn't clear whether he was defensive about the possibility that he might be disbelieved, or that

he might be believed. "I mean, I was thrown out. But I went there. I love this town."

"I *assure* you, Samuel," Nigel said, all business. "We all have a close connection to Rover's Corner. We are all proper Mainers."

"Vermonters — " Thomas said.

"I thought this town was in New Hampshire," said Ophelia, mad that the attention had shifted. "*And* I think we all know why we are here, and what the evil we face is! It's —"

"Vampires!" a helpful member of the Kiss Army said.

"Oh no," said Nigel. "It is the spirits of the Abenaki, dispossessed and driven mad. They will flay us and wear our skins over their own deathless bones in a macabre pantomime of life — "

"I'm sure," Thomas Hittler said, his voice modulated to be both loud and comforting at once, "that it is just the ghost of an old whore drowned by some Wiggleton Prep students — "

"Hey now, don't go there," Scrape said. "It's werewolves."

"No way!" It was another member of the Kiss Army, shaking with an animal rage. "Werewolves are the good guys. In fact, only by embracing our lupine natures can we fight off the ancient evil." He snatched a tablespoon out of his frappe, licked it clean, and then peered in at the curved surface of the flatware. Eyes narrowed and nostrils flared, he shook his long hair once — kind of like a Breck Girl, Sam noticed — and stared. "Be the werewolf," he muttered. "*Be* the werewolf." Nothing happened, so everyone went back to ignoring him.

"You're all wrong," said Sam. "It's not any supernatural agency at all. At least, not ultimately. It's the government, I'm sure of it." Sam commanded attention. "I think they put something in all of our frappes. That's why we're all on edge. All so nuts. I didn't drink mine. Did everyone else drink theirs?" It looked like everyone had. A few people even had pinkish, milky mustaches. Sam suddenly felt very alone.

"No," Ophelia said in a tone of voice that rolled its eyes better than any actual pair of eyes could have. "You are all wrong. Especially you!" she said, pointing an imperious finger at the first member of the Kiss Army. "We do not face mere vampires. The great evil lurking in these woods are *dham*pires. *Dham*pires, as you may not know, are the hideous spawn of a vampire and hu — " and the very beginnings of that convoluted explanation was the last thing Ophelia Darque would ever say, as at that very moment a rock came flying through the front window of Copley's, shattering it as it flew across the room and cracked the lithe young authoress right in the head. She fell into a swoon, limp and broken like a china doll. A doll with enormous breasts.

And then someone began to scream. Everyone did, really.

"ALL RIGHT, ALL right!" Shelly Johnson shouted from the doorway. "God, you people are worse than my kids." She was a large woman with facial features a size and a half too big for her head. Glasses that would have looked owlish on anyone else barely registered on her face. She hefted a paper shopping bag by the twine handles. "This is the deal. I got a bag full of rocks right here. I got a station wagon full of my nine goddamned brats a half-mile away because you bastards took up all the parking spaces. I got a cheating drunk of a husband loving up some tender young freshman right now, if that clock on the wall is right, and we've got only a few minutes to the Showdown. So are you kids going to get your acts together or what?" That "what" — *will I have to stone every one of you little turds to death like I did Morticia Addams there* — hung silently in the air like the promise of candy on Halloween.

"What is the evil we face, Ms. Johnson?" Sam asked.

"It is within," she said.

"That's right," Bart said. "Evil is always within us. Evil isn't some external thing you can just do away with via magic spells or goofy rituals. We all have our own dark sides. The Showdown isn't about monsters or ghosts, it's about us. Man's inhumanity to man." He tapped his chest. "The Showdown is in here."

"Pfft," Shelly said. She dropped her bag and raised her own hand to her face. "Actually, it's in here." She grabbed her lower lip and began to tear the flesh from her jaw. "Take this, you paperback-writin' hacks!" And from the void that was once her face spewed forth a swarm obsidian-black junebugs, filling Copley's like an evil cloud.

And Sam again began to scream. But he couldn't hear himself over the beating of wings.

LATER THAT NIGHT, a long-jawed man opened the door of Copley's, hat in hand and mumbled apologies on his lips. " — train service from Providence is ever so mercurial at this time of night. Additionally, my poor maiden aunt needed a fourth for her whist game . . ." He looked up and saw the slaughter. Bones picked clean of muscle, but not of offal or intestine. Not-quite-empty eye sockets stared back at Howard with swirling blobs of viscous fluid where well-formed irises once so closely observed the world.

"Oh," he said, and bowed his head slightly. Then he closed the door to Copley's and began to walk back home through those Cyclopean mountains that stood ageless and trackless under the bowl of the starry night. Gnarled, legend-haunted woods swayed and sagged under the whisper of distant gusting shores as Howard picked his way back to the gaslights and gabled roofs of home. As he walked, to keep himself company, he whistled like a squid. ℮

Nick Mamatas *once sought to explain a great SF master thusly: "[Name Redacted] is an asshole who writes like a dream." Saner editorial heads kept it out of print, but now these same heads suggest: Nick Mamatas is a dream who writes like an asshole.*

The Stone-Hearted Queen

BY KELLY BARNHILL

ILLUSTRATIONS BY DOREEN SALCHER

IN WHICH
DESTINY WILL
NOT BE DENIED,
OR FULFILLED

MEN CAME IN search of sons. They ripped off doors, pried boys from the hands of clutching, screeching mothers, and scattered the hay in the barns. In retrospect, we should have known they sought sons and not daughters, which is to say that my father should have known. But he did not. Men came, and my father thought they came for me.

My father heard the men approach while the rest of us lay dreaming, deep in our beds. He had been waiting, again, and unable to sleep. Unable to sleep for days. At the first intimation of hoof-beats, the first whiff of teeth and shield and unsheathed blade, my father dragged me from my bed and hauled me bodily into the garden at the south side of the house. He was old — impossibly old by then, but fear had made him strong. Magic too, most likely.

"I'm sorry," he said, "I'm so, so sorry." And with a wave of his withered hands and an agonized, lonely cry, he transformed me into a stone right in the middle of the tomato patch. He knelt beside me, laid his hands upon the cool, heavy curve of my body as it was now and whispered, "I love you. My darling, darling child. It's temporary. I can't let them find you. God knows what they'd do."

I only heard as a stone hears and felt as a stone feels. Even now, the memories are stiff, cold and inscrutable. I do remember the trembling of his hands. In his younger days, my father had quick, sure hands, deft with quill, herb and staff. He was a scholar's scholar and a magician's magician. Princes and mages sought his council (though they feared it too); colleges invited his musings; the downtrodden sought his aid. His library once rivaled the finest universities. Despite banishment (twice), imprisonment (eight attempts, though no prison could hold him), and once an advancing army, nothing could diminish his power, grace and influence. Nothing except age. In these last moments of his life, he was a misty recollection of his earlier self — and fading fast. My transformation sapped him entirely. There would be no more magic that night. And since he did not live through the night, there was no more magic at all.

As a stone, I felt the hoof beats approaching, impossibly loud. I heard them echo in the dirt, in the rock, in the pillars of the earth. As a stone, I listened to the scraping footsteps of my aged father as he made his way from the garden to the front of the house. He set his staff upon the ground and leaned upon it. I felt its power radiate from the point of contact to the core of the world and back again. I listened as it picked up echoes from the conversations of the stars. I remembered as a stone remembers: etched and permanent. The words would never leave me.

The men arrived — all iron and leather and hoof. My father slammed his staff against the ground, an action that in earlier days brought men to their knees. In the garden, I felt the staff like a slap of lightning. I felt myself shudder, vibrate and hum, and wondered if I might crack. The men did not notice and dismounted instead. From the garden I watched — patient and unblinking.

"She is gone," my father said. "She is far away and will be of no use to you. There is nothing for you here."

The heaviest man approached. I felt his footsteps. He came to the front stoop while the men behind him gathered and mobbed, trampling the flowers that my mother had lovingly planted and cultivated. The big

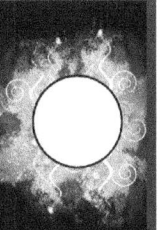

man pierced the ground with his sword and leaned upon the hilt. The big man laughed, a loud, violent laugh, and shook the ground where he stood.

"*She?*" he demanded. "What use have I for *she?* Your wife, your daughter, your mother, they are only useful after the battle is won — and don't look at me that way, old man. The battle will surely be won, and we will indeed return to — " he laughed again, "make use." He stamped and gestured to the men at his right. It was then that I saw the group of horses that still held men on their backs. Young men, no older than twenty-five, and many as young as ten. They were bound to their saddles, their mouths tied with bloody bandages. As a stone, I felt the places where their blood had soaked into the earth, where their tongues had been cut and left for the crows. After all, a good soldier doesn't talk back.

Two men picked up my father and brought him to the big man, forcing him down to his knees. Another group of clomping boots entered the house and dragged my brothers into the yard. Their hands and legs were bound and their mouths were gagged. The boys with bloody faces looked on sadly.

Stay silent, I whispered in my stone voice. *Say nothing*, I breathed my stone breath. And whether they heard me or felt me or just had the good sense to keep their mouths shut, I do not know. But they said nothing, and did not resist their binding.

My mother followed — or not so much followed as was dragged, screaming and punching, hooked under the arm of a man with a mask covering half of his face.

"So unladylike," tutted the big man. "I do hope your sons haven't picked up your poor behavior. Though if they do, we will handle it. As they say, spare the knife, spoil the soldier." They tied my brothers to the horses while the big man looked at my huddled father on the ground. "You had a chance, old man. You were *right there*, and yet you did *nothing*. I will no longer wait for your loyalty. The king will die, and with him

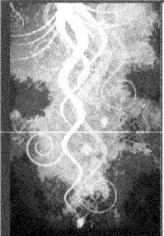

his family and court. I will do this because you lacked the courage."

"No," I yelled in my silent stone voice. "Courage had nothing to do with it. He's old. And he hates you. That's it." They could not hear me, of course, though the other stones gave me their own affirmations. I felt their agreement, their encouragement, and their love.

"You have lived a coward's life. What is magic to a sword? What is a library to an army? And you will die now like a rat at my feet." And with that he reached down, grabbed my father by his sparse hair and twisted hard. Had I been flesh, had I been standing next to him, I have no doubt that my heart would have broken in two and I would have died right there. But my heart was not flesh. My heart was stone, my flesh was stone. I heard the snap of his fragile neck, and my heart stayed whole. My father slumped to the ground. I felt the land sigh, the trees sigh, the air and stars and core of the world all sigh. As a stone, I mourned a stony grief and wept stony tears that clinked softly on the ground. Each tear was a pale pebble, the color of pearls that shone softly in the starlit night. My mother lifted her head and turned sharply towards me. She saw stone surrounded by stone tears. "Hush," she mouthed and gave me a stern look. I swallowed my tears. No more came.

The men released my mother who ran to my father, gathering his body in her arms. He was as light as grass and my mother was much younger, still fresh of face and strong. She lifted him like an infant to her breast.

The men remounted. "He is not worth burying," the big man said to my mother.

"I want my sons," my mother said. Behind the big man, my eldest brother shook his head wildly. Ever the farmer, my dear Hans. Get the wolf away, then see to regathering the lambs.

The big man tilted his head and sighed a sad sigh. "And I want a good bottle of wine and a night alone with you, but there are some things that must wait, aren't there?

Battle first, pleasure second. You will have your sons — what's left of them anyway — when we have warriors on the throne instead of scholars. Blood will out. The land needs blood and we will feed it."

"Give me my boys!" my mother shouted, but her voice was drowned by the thunder of hoofs. My mother knelt to the ground, laying my father's body on the grass and kissing his forehead, then his eyes, then his mouth. She looked back into the garden, at the stone that was me, and nodded. She went into the house and returned with a white cloth. My mother was a poet and a scholar's assistant, and while she had no gift with magic, she knew a thing or two about remedies. She laid the cloth over my stone body. Immediately, I stood, myself again, still in my night gown. My tears, however, remained as stones. I gathered them into my pocket.

My mother regarded me. "He did this?" she asked.

"Yes," I said, thinking, *why on earth would I do this to myself?* Though I said nothing. I knew a thing or two about my mother. Like when to keep my mouth closed.

"Your father," she said, "is an idiot." She nodded curtly to herself, as though putting an end to the matter, and then began to weep. Her tears surged and poured to the ground, leaving a large, damp stain on the ground. I did not cry. My heart was heavy within me, as though it had not transformed, as though it remained stone. I clutched at my stone tears instead, and grieved as a stone grieves — a silent, unmoving weight.

Together, we carried my father into the house and buried him the next day.

WHEN MY MOTHER married my father, she was a fraction of his age, a child, practically. My mother was a poet, celebrated before she could walk. She made verses in her cradle, and coaxed stanzas into song as she could grip a lute. Her words pierced souls, her phrasing dazzled the ear. Her voice was astonishing and pure. People gathered from every country, kingdom and tribe to listen to the voice of the child poet. Regardless of language or creed, people understood and were moved to tears. When the King, Emperor, High Priest and Lord Executioner of her nation began to feel that her work had become too political, he banned poetry, and after poetry he banned singing, and when that wasn't enough he banned the exposure to books by children under the age of fourteen. After that, he signed the execution order of one Aline Beringar, my mother.

Thanks to a network of underground scholars and writers and revolutionaries, my mother was spirited away and hidden in the great library at my father's house, where she was given a new name and occupation. She catalogued his books, kept careful track of items acquired, loaned and borrowed, and took charge of his correspondence, which, alas, was in a dreadful state. She planted a garden and harvested and preserved, laying meals on the table that sustained my father in a way that he had never been sustained before, making him feel strong, satiated and utterly satisfied. She was a sweet thing, my mother, lovely of face, but whose goodness was so genuine and natural that beauty could never pollute it, and my father loved her in the way that he felt he ought — protective, paternal, like a beloved uncle. And though he knew he would miss her desperately would she ever to go, he knew it was right and proper for lovely young maidens to find suitable husbands and thus he kept himself aware of single men who might be worthy suitors for his beloved Aline. The trouble was, they all were too dim, or too self-centered, or too imbecilic, or too utterly, utterly wicked. He told himself that he would continue to look, but he knew it would be a long, long time before the right one came along.

My mother, meanwhile, had other plans.

Each day, after her duties in the library had been completed, she went into the woods and sang verses to the trees. As she sang, she removed her shoes and laid the

pads of her feet on the soft and welcoming moss on the forest floor. In truth, she missed having an audience. She missed their faces, their looks of pleasure and joy and epiphany and love. She missed that moment when someone's view had changed — an alteration invisible to most, but my mother saw it. When she sang to the trees, they enjoyed it. She could feel their pleasure in her feet. She sang of the cruelties of the warrior king that continued to ravage the land that was once her home. She sang the old songs of a peasantry that gathered together to move the hands of princes, and thus alter their place in history. She sang songs of an old scholar whose face looked like love.

One day, my father, restless in his study, left the house for a walk. As he wandered through the wood, he heard a voice that he thought at first was a bird, and then thought it was an angel. He listened to a story of a maiden far from home who loved a man that couldn't see her. He wept for that poor, invisible maiden. He removed his shoes to listen better. With his bare feet

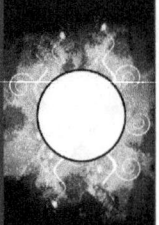

upon the cool moss, he caught sight of my mother, her face flushed with singing, her black hair unbound and falling like water down her strong back, pooling over the length of her skirts.

This was a magic that had no remedy. They were married by the end of the week.

MY BROTHERS WERE born within the year. Hans, an hour older and twice as big, had the broad feet, broad hands and broad back of a farmer. As he grew, he tended the animals (all of which were sleek and fat under his hands) and coaxed food from the ground in ways that my mother never could. Stephen, whose large, gray eyes grew larger every year with reading, until, owl-like, he could see in the dark, was drawn to my father's library from the time he was able to walk. By the time he was two, he was reading texts. By the time he was ten he was drafting exegeses and opinions which, not once but four times, had been labeled heretical. My father beamed with pride. But neither had my father's *other* gifts.

I had those. Small, underdeveloped, sickly me.

Despite my size, or perhaps because of it, I was a miracle. Five times after my brothers were born, my mother's waist began to swell with twins, and five times the twins were lost before they ever quickened in her womb. After my parents had given up any hope of new children, they went out into the field after the boys were asleep to commiserate and comfort. My mother whispered verses to the grass and to the stars. My father transformed rocks into singing birds, birds into angels. He wound flowers in her hair and tried desperately to please her. In the darkness they sighed and sorrowed, kissed and groaned, and in so doing conceived me. A singleton. And I lived.

Though I was scrawny, blue and squalling, my parents loved me and my brothers doted on me.

A poet, sang my mother.

A magician, whispered my father.

Hans brought pumpkins and corn and dried flowers into the nursery. He told me stories of the ducks and cows and goats. Stephen read me treatises and theses and ream upon ream of dusty parchment. My mother wrote verses on the walls, on the floors and ceilings too. And when she ran out of room, she traced verses on my skin, across my forehead, and on the soles of my feet. My father conjured — at first pretty things that might please a child: a flower from a bead, a yellow bird from a half-gnawed cracker. Later, he showed me the spinning world, the revolution of the moon, the burning sun in a multitude of burning suns.

When I was three, I traced a verse into the silky mud of the spring fields and the seedlings began to sing. People gathered on the road before my father bustled out of his study to shut them up.

When I was five, I began to tell a story to a child in the village about a duck with a woman's face, only to see a duck with a woman's face swimming in the pond. My mother hastily shooed both daughter and duck home for a quick lesson on subtlety.

When I was six and a half, soldiers arrived when I was playing in the yard, demanding to know where my father's loyalties lay. I barely noticed the soldiers, but focused my attention on the pile of brightly colored pebbles next to the garden. I found that all matter is the same matter, which is to say that all things on earth come from the same spark. I found that a pebble could be the same as a butterfly, which could be the same as a toad. It all depended on how you looked at it. I picked up a small stone. It was red and green, and felt cool with a pleasing heft in my hand. Then I looked at it again. It was a butterfly, red, green, cool, light, and gone.

The men talking to my father raised their voices until they were shouting. I barely noticed, but marveled at the butterflies coming thick and fast from the rapidly diminishing pile of stones. I didn't notice the thunder of boots. For all I know, the stones may have tried to warn me, but I couldn't hear them. Not yet anyway.

"Am I to assume," the soldier said, "that she inherited her father's capabilities?" The butterflies rose and scattered. I scrambled to my feet and hid my hands behind my back and hung my head. Like all children, I knew how to look remorseful, even when I did not know yet what I had done.

"No," my father said quickly, bending down to pick me up. I heard his bones crack and groan under my weight. "None of my children are endowed. My son raises butterflies for pollination. She's a naughty girl to lure them with sugar. We've spoken to her about this, and yet she continues — Aline!" He called to my mother. "Aline!" His voice spiked in panic, and without knowing why, I started to cry.

"Interesting," the soldier said. "*Interesting.*"

That night, we gathered the possessions we needed and all the books we could carry into the cart, harnessed the mules, tethered the milk-goats, and tearfully left everything else behind. A few of my father's friends were able to smuggle out a few more books and the rest of the animals, but the last we heard, the soldiers came back and burned our beautiful library to the ground.

After that, I was forbidden to work magic. Or poetry. They were both too dangerous.

THE GROUND WAS thick and heavy with the remains of winter and the promises of spring. My mother and I took turns digging, and though we were both strong, the sheer weight of each shovel full made our muscles stretch and clench until it seemed they would rip off. As we got deeper, the weight in my chest became more pronounced. Each time I leaned in, it was harder to pull myself out. Even my mother noticed it.

"How is it possible?" she asked. I shrugged. I had no idea. I did not tell her that when I laid my hand on my chest I could not feel the beating of my heart. It was a silent as any stone.

After anointing my father with human tears (my mother's) and a stone tear (mine), we laid him down and covered him over. In a month, my mother would plant an apple tree over the spot where he lay. In a year, she would harvest apples that tasted like honey and wine, that led people to poetry, to love, to holy truth. People said that apple tree would stand at that spot for a hundred years. I have no way of knowing if it would or not, but I still like to believe it to be true.

By mid afternoon, I packed my rucksack with a day's water and wine and meat, belted my father's sword around my hips and slid sheathed daggers into my boots. My mother blocked the door.

"You're not going." She said this without conviction.

"I am," I said, and kissed her on her cheek. I had to stand on tip toe. At fifteen, one would think that I would have reached her height, but I hadn't grown in three years, and remained stuck below her chin.

"You're an idiot, too," she said, with a curt nod that again settled the matter.

I shrugged. "Maybe," I said.

I WENT OUTSIDE. Warriors, as a rule, are easy to follow. They leave a wide, trampled swath that can be seen from the ground as well as the air. Crows gathered along their trail, followed by sparrows, followed by doves. Their horses and cart wheels dug deeply into the soft, impressionable spring ground. I bent down to touch the hoof prints. The mud shimmered in the trampled grass. It smelled like life. And death. Which side I would be on at the end of the day I did not know, nor did I care.

My mother came out of the door, her eyes and nose red rimmed and raw. "Wait," she said. "Take this." She held my father's staff. I held up my hands.

"I can't," I said. "He never taught me how to use it."

She shrugged. "No one taught him either. Anyway, perhaps it won't matter. If they think you can use it, perhaps that's enough."

And with that, she tied it to my rucksack, kissed me on each eye and my mouth and ran into the house. Inside the house, she whispered poetry, quietly, constantly, under her breath. As I walked, then ran, down the warriors' track, I could still hear her. At every turn, I heard poetry. And even though she has been gone for years now, I hear it still.

ON THE FIRST night, I slept in the communal barn of six peasant farmers whose farms pinwheeled out of a central cluster of small houses. Each family had sons taken — one lost all six. Eight of the boys — and they were boys — had struggled and yelled and were relieved of their tongues. One grandmother gathered the tongues to bury them properly, and after doing so had lain down and died. I asked them to show me the spot where the boys had been cut, and they showed me eight bloody spots on the ground. I bent down, scraped up the bloody dirt and kept it in the sack with my stone tears.

In the morning, the farmers arrived with bread and milk. They squatted on the ground as I ate in silence.

Finally, a farmer with a ginger-colored beard sprinkled pleasingly with silver, spoke. "The staff you carry," he said. "It's his staff."

I nodded. "Yes," I said.

"So he is dead."

"Yes."

"So all is lost."

"Yes," I said. But the stones in my sack began to hum impatiently. "Or not," I said. "Miracles happen." I shrugged, hoping it would look convincing.

The farmer nodded and went into the barn, coming back with a horse, a chestnut gelding, who had clearly seen better days, but honestly would be better than nothing. He lashed on a saddle as well as a bow and quiver. "For the event of a miracle," he said. "A scholar king was bad enough. A warrior king is worse for farmers. How can we farm without sons?" He pointed to the staff with his chin. "Do you know how to use it?

"No," I said, blushing in shame.

"Well, it isn't doing you a bit of good on your back. Hold it in your hands. That's what he used to do."

I untied the staff and held it in both hands. It vibrated slightly, but seemed otherwise silent. I lifted it up, and, like my father, plunged it to the ground. It sang in my bones, in the ground, in the sky, and in my cold, stone heart. I heard the sky, land, rock and water all speaking with the same voice. And it was my voice.

"I need an army," I said, and whether I said this to the farmer or the sky or the very stones, I do not know. My voice came from the soles of my feet. It was dark and cool like moss, or poetry, or love songs. "An army," I said again, and the staff hummed and itched in my hands. I didn't wait for an answer, but instead scrambled onto the saddle and clucked the horse into a gallop.

THEY SAY THAT the first kings were farmers. Which is to say, the first farmers were kings. Queens too, if the stories can be believed. When I was young, I did not believe the stories — many of them were forbidden to me anyway, as my parents worried that poetry might leak, unbidden, into my mouth, and then where would we be? I learned to ignore, to keep us safe, and to unbelieve when the believing was impolitic.

Still.

There was a story — don't ask me how I know it. I could not tell you. What I know is this: Eight days before my mother was secreted out of her country, she earned the ire of the warrior king with a story. She was gathering apples. All the girls in the town were gathering apples. It was part of an old, time-honored (which is to say, most people had long since forgotten what it meant) tradition of sending the unmarried girls into the orchards to fill basket full of apples which would be pressed and fermented until the whole town was drunk on sweetness and wine and harvest, and ripe girls gathering ripe fruit to their fragrant chests, smooth and heavy and delicious. At some point in the festivities, my mother, her basket and apron spilling over with firm and soft and rotting fruit, leaned against the side of the barn, russet leaves clinging to her hair, alfalfa hanging from her skirt and she told a story. The story of the Stone Queen. It is the only story I know.

There once was a queen who was a farmer. And while all queens were farmers and all farmers were queens, this was the First Queen, and the First Farmer. Where she stepped, grain sprouted and ripened, its tender stalks weighted down. Where she laid down, ewes lambed and heifers calved and mares produced fouls with eyes like stars. The queen was a good queen, generous and fair. She gathered seed and shared with those who had nothing. She encouraged the migration of winged insects and birds and under her hands, her lands grew rich with food and animal and children.

The queen had two husbands which she kept in two houses. One husband was a scholar whose need for books was so insatiable that the queen ordered eight barns constructed for the housing and preservation of his books. Every day the queen brought him gifts of bread and cheese and skins of wine, and every day the scholar would read to her or engage her mind in the intricacies of mathematics or cosmology or grammar. It was a good marriage and a good life and they both were happy.

The second husband was a warrior, whose need for horses and weaponry were so insatiable that she constructed eight barns just to house them all. Each day the warrior husband rode off in search of conquest and adventure, and each day he came home, bloodied and breathless and she gave him gifts of bread and cheese and skins of wine. He accepted her gifts gratefully and told her stories of honor and valor and good war. It was a good marriage and they both were happy.

For a while.

But the scholar looked out on the lands and how the people looked to the queen for

their answers and thought it is not right for a simple farmer to give answers to the people.

And the warrior looked out onto the lands and saw that the people looked to the queen for protection and safety and thought it is not right for a mere woman to provide protection and safety.

And on that day, the warrior and the scholar met in secret and began to scheme.

The queen did not know of their scheming. What she did know is that the ewes stopped lambing, milk dried up in the teats of the heifers, and her favorite foal, the one with stars in its eyes, died in the noonday sun amid the fields of shriveling grain. Children starved, mothers could not nurse, and husbands turned away from their lonely wives.

Those who were angry joined the armies of the warrior husband. Those who were grieving joined the armies of the scholar husband. And the armies grew until they marched across the barren fields to the slumped figure of the queen.

"Your people do not want you," said the scholar husband. "Your answers are cir-

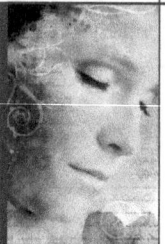

cuitous and vague and lacking in subtlety. They need a king, and that king is me."

The warrior husband nodded and elbowed him out of the way. "Your people do not want you," the warrior said. "Your protection has not protected and your powers have proved useless. They need a king, and that king is me."

The queen hung her head. Her husbands smiled, assuming that she accepted defeat, but she was only thinking. "If I can convince them otherwise," she said quietly, her mouth tilted to the ground. "If I can make them trust me again, will you give up your claim? If I can promise them that the land will give them grain and milk and meat by the end of the day, will you lay down your swords?"

The scholar and the warrior agreed, and she turned to the people. "My friends," she said, "look at your feet. What do you see?"

"Stones," the people yelled, baring their teeth.

"Then we will use stones. Please, everyone, reach down and take a stone. If you can, take two. Those with aprons, gather stones in your aprons. Those with pockets, stuff stones into your pockets."

The queen walked into the fields and the people followed her, burdened with stones.

"Here," the queen said. "Plant your stones."

The people looked around incredulously, but did as they were told. They knelt in the dirt and buried their stones.

"Now," the queen said. "Sleep." And everyone slept. Everyone except the warrior and the scholar. Creeping across the sleeping figures, they came and stood over the place where the queen lay.

"She'll trick us," they said. "She'll turn them against us."

They unsheathed their swords and sliced off her head. Then her tongue, her hands and feet, each breast, each strand of golden hair. They buried each piece separately, so as to prevent her ghost from re-associating and coming back. They let her blood soak into the ground.

When the people woke, the stones had sprouted. They became green orchards, endless millet, murky rice pallets, succulent vegetables, and miles and miles of wheat. Milk flowed, animals bloated with young, and children came back into the arms of their mothers. The people looked for the queen to thank her, but she was gone. They called her name but she did not answer. The scholar and the warrior tried to tell them that it was for the best, but the people did not listen. They wept and mourned and prayed. They threw themselves into their farms and families, hoping to draw the queen back with abundant life.

They wait for her still.

WHEN I ARRIVED at the castle, the king was already dead. He had probably been dead for a day. His body was strung from the outer wall, limp and blue and naked. The horse beneath me shuddered and quaked, and I dismounted, bringing my nose to his nose.

"Thank you," I said. "And I'm sorry. Rest and go home. You'll find your way."

The armies still loyal to the dead king made war on the armies of the big man and his hungry band of big men. The big men rode on horses. On the ground were scattering boys, some with swords, many with sticks, all with bloody rags wrapped around their mouths. I did not see my brothers. I did not doubt that they were there. Overhead, masses of crows, lured by the stink of battle spiraled and twined, waiting for the masses of meat — both dead and mostly dead — that waited deliciously on the blood-soaked dirt. I thought of my father, crumpled on the ground, now part of the ground.

"Ah," a voice said behind me. "A girl. I've seen prettier, of course, but you'll do." I turned. The man with the leather mask on his face emerged from the trees. He was big, colossally so. His chest was bound with leather and iron, as were his boots. His sword was unsheathed, and so sharp it sang in the air as though slicing it cleanly in half.

"You don't seem to be fighting," I said,

yanking at my own sword. It was stuck slightly in its sheathing, from so many years of disuse. The staff I had retied tightly on my back so as not to lose it. I did not dare untie it now. "Frightened are we?"

He scoffed and narrowed his eyes. "Do I know you, girl?"

"I don't think so," I said and made a stab at his shoulder. I missed of course and was thrown off balance. He laughed.

"Poor thing. Poor little thing. Did we think we were going to be a brave girl today? I suppose you have a brother down there." He tutted. His lips, through their hole in his mask, were big and thick and purple. "My, my. How awfully stupid."

I slashed again with my sword, this time hitting his blade with a sharp tang. The sound of metal on metal rang through my bones, rattled my teeth, hummed against my cold, stone heart. And in this moment, I saw him as a stone sees. He was a baby, a man, a dead man, all at once. He was flesh and soft and laughably weak. The staff on my back, without my touching it, grew hot. It hummed and vibrated and whispered. Under my feet, the stones whispered too.

"What the hell is that," the man demanded.

"I hear nothing," I said, as the stones told me what to do. I dropped to my knees. "Please," I begged. "Please don't kill me." My eyes did not tear, but my lips quivered. I laid the sword on the grass and lifted up my hands.

The man relaxed and smiled. "Well that depends my dear. Are you going to make it worth my while?" The voices of the stones grew louder until they screeched under my knees. I smiled at the man in the mask and tilted my head. He grabbed me by the front of my tunic and lifted me up. With both hands I grabbed the daggers from my boots and slid each one neatly into his belly. He gasped, brought my cheek to his face. His breath was pale and dry and cool. Like a stone. I felt it flow out, fade, and disappear as he slumped down to the earth, a crumpled, lifeless heap.

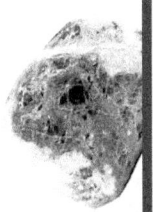

"Sorry," I said. And I meant it. I pulled the staff off of my back. It was still hot. I walked down the hill into the battle field. I saw as a stone sees and felt as a stone feels. Under my feet, the grass, the dirt, the rock, the pillars of the earth, all whispered and sang. Poetry first, then battle songs. Though really, aren't they the same?

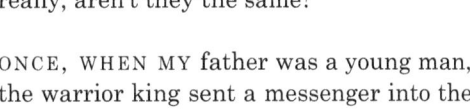

ONCE, WHEN MY father was a young man, the warrior king sent a messenger into the depths of the library.

"Your presence," the messenger said. "Now."

Sometimes, when I imagine my father that young, he looks like Stephen. Other times he looks like Hans. Or my mother. Or me. Regardless, he was young enough, he likely was smooth-faced, small-boned, more child than man. He left his books still opened, his pages uncategorized and unfinished.

"You." The warrior king sat on a throne made from bent swords, molded shields and carved bone.

"Yes sir," my father said. And though his voice trembled, though his face was pale, his heart did not quake inside of him. Even that young, his power was great, and he knew it.

"You seek to overthrow me I assume."

"No, sir," my father said truthfully. "I don't."

"And you would lie to a king." The king stood, raised his sword, and placed its tip on my father's chest, an inch above his heart. The blade shimmered in the candle light, and bored through the pale muslin. Slowly, a dark red rose bloomed. My father swallowed but his mouth was dry.

"No sir," he replied. "I would not lie to a king."

"I will ask this once," the king said. "And if I do not like the answer, I will slice your throat, and will then cut out your heart and feed it to the crows. Yesterday, someone translated an incendiary text — a worthless, pitiful excuse for falsified folklore. That someone tacked the document in the market square. And now, those who can read are

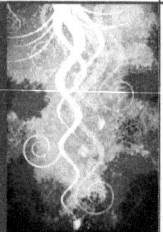

telling these — *lies*, this *heresy* — to those who cannot. And now all I hear is a mythical Stone Queen and her magical beasts. Do you deny that this person was you?"

"Not at all," my father said. His voice still quaked. His hands still shook. But his breathing was easy and gentle. His mouth made words, but his other mouth, the mouth in his head and in his cool, still heart, made something else entirely. *Sleep*, said the mouth in his head. *Sleep*, said the mouth in his heart. "I discovered the text in my translations, and was moved by its tender descriptions of our primitive forebears." The king swayed slightly, and touched the tip of his sword on the marble floor, resting his weight upon the hilt. But the tip slipped and the king staggered.

"I shall sit," said the king, and he swayed back to his seat.

Sleep, said my father's other mouth. The king yawned. "Once upon a time," murmured my father, and the king's eyes started to droop. "All kings were farmers and all farmers were kings." And the king slept.

My father did not return to his desk, but went to his horse instead, riding swiftly to the land of the scholar king where the university welcomed him with satisfaction and relief.

NO ONE NOTICED me as I returned to the castle. The battle raged and men and horses fell. I raised my staff to the sky. It hummed and sang. My hands began to blister and peel, yet I still hung on. I heard the language of the sky, the stones, the birds, and the core of the earth. And the words were the same, and the words were mine. I called out — a single, rasping cry, and brought my staff to the ground with a loud crack. The sky flashed and poured and the men looked up.

"Birds," I yelled. And there were birds. Just the crows at first, but then sparrows and doves, then hawks and eagles and herons and turkeys. They swooped and scurried and pecked. They made off with swords, confused archers, and flew in the faces of men bent on blood. With my staff on the ground, I could hear things that I could not hear before. I could hear my mother singing war songs as she gathered the farmers together. I could here men and women of the villages armed with whatever they could find marching towards the castle of the scholar king.

They sang the song of the Stone Queen.

The big man saw me with the staff and reared his horse.

"Well, well," he said. "I believe the young lady is confused. We have no need for magicians here. The land needs blood, not some girl mumbling magic words." He rode towards me, his poor horse foaming and panting, its eyes bloodshot and wild.

I did not move from my spot, but instead reached into my bag and pulled out a handful of the bloody dirt. When he was close enough, I reached back and threw it into his face. He fell from his horse, and after rolling backwards a few times, staggered up, desperately clawing at his eyes.

"What is this," he bellowed. "Get it out, get it — dear god. Dear *God*. No! Not the knife! Not the — " He pawed at the bloody dirt, then at the air around him, then at his mouth. As he screamed, blood dripped, then poured from the corners of his mouth. He tried to speak, but he could not. His tongue was gone.

I turned away. "Stones," I yelled. And there were stones. They rolled from the hillside, and birthed themselves from the dirt under our feet. Eight stones rolled over the big man, and continued to roll. Anyone brandishing his sword was crushed. Anyone who dropped his sword was spared.

I dropped my staff, utterly spent.

The boys with bloody mouths walked away from their battle places and wandered towards me. Hans was there, Stephen too. Hans was missing a few teeth, Stephen, his left hand. Both stared at me silently, their faces dark with dried blood.

ONCE, WHEN MY mother was out, my father took me out to the forest to tell me about magic. I was twelve years old and impatient and exasperated. Magic, if it existed at all, was clearly an occupation for old men, and my father was the oldest of them all. I dawdled, and sighed, tried to make a show of not listening.

"Listen," my father said. "There is nothing I can teach you. Absolutely nothing. It cannot be taught. It is simply instinct. When you are faced with a situation, your first instinct is probably right. This is important."

I shrugged. I didn't believe him.

THE FARMERS ARRIVED at the outer lip of the western hills. They saw me with my staff and their bloody, ruined sons. They did not move.

The boys without tongues gathered round me. They touched my face, my hair, my hands. Their faces were silent and sad and very, very old. The staff in my hands began to hum once again.

I knelt on the ground, told the boys to kneel too. Then I told them to lay down. I gathered what was left of the bloody dirt into my hands and scattered it on the ground in front of my knees. The stones under my feet sang quietly. A slow sad song. The sky above my head whispered encouragement.

"I need a knife," I said. "I left mine up there."

It would have been easier, of course, if the knife was sharper, but sometimes you use what's available. After three tries, my tongue lay on the mound of bloody dirt. I tried hard not to cough or vomit. The boys looked so peaceful lying there. So peaceful and so sleepy. My stone heart was heavy within me. Heavy and cool and quiet. I laid down. Later, I remember thinking that I was a stone again in the tomato patch. That my father was there and alive, that my mother whispered a poem — something long and sweet and tender. Something called the Stone Queen. When I woke, I heard the sound of singing. It sounded like angels, like birds, like angels who wish they were birds.

It sounded like Hans. Or perhaps it was Stephen. Or perhaps, it was me.

THEY CALLED HER *the Silent Queen while she was alive and the Stone Hearted Queen after she had died. While the years prior to her birth, and the years leading up to her eventual crowning had been marked by violence, her reign was peaceful, as were the two centuries following her death. If the accounts are to be believed, she governed in total silence, due to a battle wound that left her without the power of speech. And while she relied heavily on the assistance of her two brothers, in all accounts available in that period, there was no doubt that the citizenry looked to their queen for leadership and guidance.*

The stories get strange, of course, when it comes to the matter of her heart. In no fewer than eighty-two accounts of the Silent Queen, people make reference to the fact that her heart is not flesh, but stone. This is further odd because fifty-seven documents attest that at the point of her death her body became stone and her heart, finally, became flesh. This would have been discounted as mere myth, were it not for the fact that the Silent Queen, or the Stone Hearted Queen, if you will, is not buried in the castle crypt along with her brothers, her mother, and the subsequent royal family. Instead there is a statue of an old woman with a crown, presumably a rendering of the queen in her later years, holding a rough-hewn staff. Even today, five hundred years later, many people attest to that if one is to put one's ear on her chest, that a faint beating can be heard. Like that of a human heart. ☙

Kelly Barnhill *is an author in Minneapolis, Minn. Her latest children's books are* Monsters of the Deep *and* Animals with No Eyes, *both released in January 2008 by Captstone Press. She is online at www.kellybarnhill.com.*

Ganaranok's Lament

A SHAKESPEAREAN LOVE STORY BY RORY STEVES

Rory Steves lives in Ohio, and works in a five-state area delivering groceries to your finer inner-city stores.

Ganaranok wept, his tears flowed down his face and created a small pool next to his fourth foot on the left side, the one with the hangnail that he had never been able to completely chew away. All six of his arms flailed at the mushroom he leaned his blue millipede body against; little pieces of the mushroom formed a small pile by the 14th, 15th, and 16th feet on his right side, the ones with that stubborn rash.

Naranite had never said a word, not once, about the rash or the hangnail, they had never mattered to her. Oh, sweet Naranite, never again to see the three suns reflect off of her luminous pink segments. Grief shook the entire length of his body; sorrow filled his hearts, all four of them.

Why? Why? His weeping continued, how by all the thousand knees of the Bringer could this have happened? The pain filling his soul was so great he thought of drowning himself in the lake, but he was fearful that the fish might reach him before he joined the Taker. He was also certain he would strangle the Taker when he arrived for even conceiving of so heinous a fate for him.

He paused his silent wailing when he heard his name called, and the voice calling his name was female. The voice called again.

It was Lacintana, brood sister to his beloved Naranite. She moved close to him and gently licked away his tears. Then she suddenly flexed her segments and bumped him, a bump that could mean only one thing! Ganaranok blinked his twelve eyes in surprise; he never even suspected!

She began the dance, the dance that would culminate in the mating ritual. He was enthralled as he watched the moon chain's reflections dance along her sinuous multi-segmented body. Grief and sorrow vanished as he began his part of the dance.

Lacintana knew she would always miss her sister, but now Ganaranok was available, and she had always thought he was the most virile of all males.

The mating had lasted long into the night, causing Ganaranok to awaken late in the morning; the light of all three suns warmed his face.

He looked over at Lacintana, still sleeping, so beautiful. He rose and stretched, preparing himself for his dance of joy.

He began his dance, weaving, coiling, racing up to the top of a mushroom and jumping — this took a great deal of coordination — to the top of another.

He spared a glance to his beloved, Lacintana was awake and watching him with pride; most males got themselves all tangled up when they tried to jump.

He danced a weaving path to the rock he had selected and raced up it as fast as his thousand feet could run. His hearts, all four of them, were filled with joy as he leapt out, his arms spread wide.

And was snatched up in the beak of Kurak the Iridescent Bluebird. Tasty, Kurak thought as he chewed, very tasty. ☙

The Difficulties of Evolution

BY KAREN HEULER

ILLUSTRATION BY STEVEN ARCHER

IN WHICH FISH
GOTTA SWIM,
BIRDS GOTTA FLY
& MAMA'S GOT A
BRAND NEW BAG

I WANT TO SAVE this one," Franka said, stroking Yagel, her youngest. The child sat in Franka's lap, her dark eyes following the doctor happily. She chattered and waved her small hands around.

"She's my second," Franka added. Her hand rubbed the spot on Yagel's ribs where it was thickening.

"Ah, yes," Dr. Bennecort said. "Evan. What was he — ten or so — when it started?"

"Yes. I thought, at her age, it was too early, there should be lots of time."

"You know it can happen at any point. I had a patient who was sixty . . . "

"Yes, you told me," Franka said impatiently, and stopped herself. She took a moment to calm herself, and the doctor waited. He was good — patient, professional — and Franka hoped that he could help. She wanted to say, "I'm imagining the worst," and have him reply, "The worst won't happen." She knew better, but she was hoping to hear it nevertheless.

IT HAD HAPPENED suddenly. Franka was bathing her daughter the week before, cooing at the smiling, prattling wonder of her life. After the shock of watching Evan go, she knew she was a little possessive. Franka smoothed the washcloth over the toddler's skin, gently swirling water over the perfect limbs, the wrinkles at the joints, the plum calves and shoulders. She felt a thickening at the ribs — an area that, surely, just the day before had been soft and pliant.

She automatically talked back as Yagel babbled, but she felt her face freeze and Yagel noticed the difference in her touch and grew concerned, her legs pumping impatiently.

And Franka couldn't keep her hands off her, touching, touching the spots that were changing, until Yagel began to bruise, and Simyon told her to go to the doctor. He said it coldly. He felt the spots that Franka felt, and he holed himself up deep inside, leaving Franka to find out the truth alone.

"She's my second," Franka whispered to the doctor. He'd been highly recommended by Deirdre, who had three emerald beetles tethered to her house, buzzing and smacking the picture window when the family sat down to watch TV. "We know their favorite shows," Dierdre said. "We know when they're happy."

Franka didn't want Yagel to end up like that, a child-sized insect swooping to her and away, eating from her palm. She wanted Yagel to end up a little girl.

"Time will tell," Dr. Bennecort said. Time, and blood tests. Yagel screamed when the needle went in, but she forgot it all when given a lollipop. Maybe everything was still all right.

A month to get the results. And packets of information, numbers of people to talk to, a video explaining the process. He forgot she already had all this, from when Evan changed.

She didn't look at any of it, and neither did Simyon.

"I don't want this to happen," Franka whispered to her daughter, day and night. Yagel cooed back.

"Don't you think you could love her, no matter what?" Deirdre asked cruelly when she came to lend her support. She so seldom left her home; she preferred to stay close to her emerald boys. Some people let their children go when they changed, gave in and released them. Took the ones that swam to the sea, and the ones that flew to the hills. The lucky ones kept the cats and dogs as pets — not such a change, after all — and put the ponies in the yard. You could wish for the higher orders; you could wish for the softer, cuddlier evolutions, but you couldn't change what was meant to be.

"But whatever they are, you love them, still," Deirdre said.

THE THREE EMERALD beetles were about the size of a five-year-old child. They lifted and fluttered up and hit the window sometimes three at a time, with whirring thuds, they pulled to the ends of their cords, their green wings pulsing.

"My dears, my sweets," Deirdre thought as she stood on the inside of the picture window, her fingertips touching the glass as they swooped towards her, their hard black eyes intent. "My all, my all, my all."

She put out bowls for them, rotted things mixed with honey and vitamins, her own recipe, and rolled down the awning in case it rained, and went to Franka's house when she called, where she found her friend with her child in her arms.

"Feel this," Franka said. She rubbed a spot along Yagel's ribs. "It's thicker, isn't it? Not like the rest of her skin."

Deirdre took her fingers and delicately felt the spot. It felt like a piece of tape under the skin — less resilient, forming a kind of half-moon. "Yes," Deirdre said. "Maybe. It could be anything."

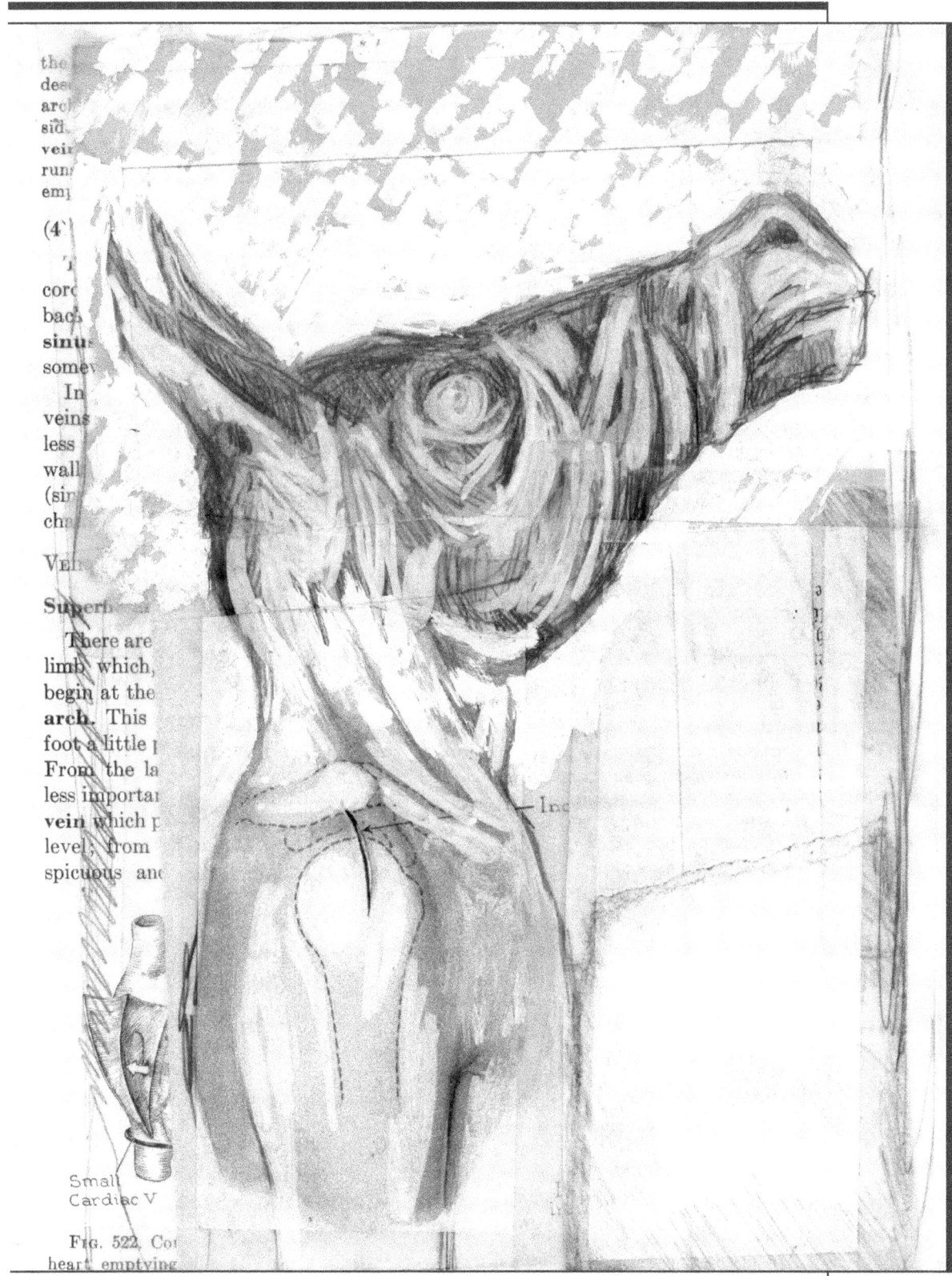

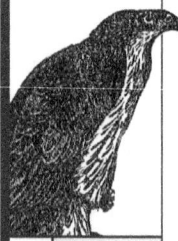

"Evan was ten," Franka whispered. "And she's only three. Your boys — did it happen at the same age for each?"

Deirdre shook her head. "Every one was different," she said, trying to find the right thing to say. "They're always different."

EVERY DAY, YAGEL'S skin thickened, making her arms and legs appear shorter. She no longer tried to stand up: crawling seemed to be more efficient. The first thick spot on her back now had a scale-like or plate-like appearance. Franka went to the library and began to look through books for an animal that matched: armadillo, no; rhino, no. And not elephant skin either. She skipped over whole sections, refusing to look at tortoises, lizards, snakes.

They were taught evolution as children, of course — the intimate, intricate link of the stages of life. Ameba, fish, crawling fish, reptile; pupa, insect; egg, bird; chimp, ape, human; all the wonderful trigonometry of form and function. The beauty of it was startling. However life started, it changed. You were a baby once, then you're different. Each egg had its own calling; no one stopped.

How beautiful it was to watch as characteristics became form, as the infant with a lithe crawl became a cat; as the toddler with the steady gaze became an owl, as the child who ran became a horse. It was magnificent. Her own brother had soared into the sky finally, a remarkable crow (always attracted to sparkle, rawkishly rowdy). She had envied him — his completion. She had stayed a child.

Still. Maybe it was less than magnificent when it was your own child. Or it was some deficit of her own. Simyon told her gruffly, "Babies grow up, Franka. You know they change. You don't decide when it's time for them to go; they do. When it's right for them. Not for you."

He was not a sympathetic man—but had that always been true? No. He used to be interested in her worries; he used to want to soothe her rather than lecture. Although— she told herself — he was dealing with it, too.

Both children evolving; leaving. So quickly gone. Of course it was hard for him, too.

She remembered her own brother's metamorphosis as a magical time—she had leapt up out of bed each morning to see the change in him overnight: a pouty mouth to a beak; dark fuzz on his shoulders into feathers; the way his feet cramped into claws; the tilt of his head and the glitter of his eye. It had been wonderful to see him fly, leaning out the window one minute, through it the next.

Even in the memory of it she heard her mother's faltering cry. How stodgy her mother had seemed.

She leaned over Yagel. "I will always love you," she confided to the child's tender ear. Yagel poked her tongue out, clamped her arms to her side. "Always," Franka repeated. "Always." She kissed her on the neck and bit her ear tenderly.

Her neighbor Phoebe had two girls, neither of them evolved. She looked pregnant again and Franka went over to talk to her. "I think Yagel is evolving," she said. "You're so lucky." Of course it was wrong not to accept her children as they were, but she felt it in her, a deep reluctance to let go.

Phoebe nodded. "It's so nice to have them at home for so long, yes. Of course there's so much beauty in the changes — you know Hildy's girl?" Franka nodded. "A lunar moth. Elegant, curved wings. Extraordinary. Trembling on the roof. Hildy's taken photos and made an incredible silkscreen image. It's haunting. I look at some of the changes and it feels almost religious."

Phoebe's face looked dutiful and Franka knew a lie when she heard one: the false sincerity, the false envy. It was always better to have children who stayed children, and not some phenomenal moth. And when they changed, there was always a judgment. No one really said it, but it was there. The mothers of sharks would always weep. Children who didn't evolve were more of a blessing, no matter how basic it was to evolve.

"You're too possessive," Simyon said, hunched over his dinner. He was eating quickly, tearing at his food. "Life is change." He finished his meal and prowled down the hall, going into his daughter's room, sniffing and blinking. "Reptile," he said, coming back. "Cold blood." He went off to watch his TV.

She drove around the next day, slowly. There were cages everywhere, some of them immense and gothic. There were new ponds, and short bursts of trees. A huge, exquisite ceramic beehive stood next to a garage. She heard the trumpet of an elephant down the next road, and the scream of a peacock.

As she drove, heads poked from the corners of garages and from behind gazebos, some of them not yet completely determined. She made a mental note to remember where they were, in case she needed them. For Yagel.

Sometimes the changes were slow, and sometimes the changes were fast. Yagel stood up again and walked like a little girl— stubby, but a little girl. She described every event of her day, repeating the things the other little girls had done, describing how one of them grew a bandit mask on her face and sometimes washed her food before eating.

"She's all right," Simyon said stubbornly.

"I'm afraid for her," she said, and her voice sounded thick. Simyon's hard, bushy eyes stared at her, ticking down her body, studying her.

Maybe Yagel would never change; maybe this was just her version of a little girl. Some evolved early; some evolved late. Every morning she counted Yagel's fingers and toes, and then she counted her own. She longed for nighttime and the rise of the wind, for the moment of freshness at the start of a storm.

She was beginning to sense her own change and was surprised one day to look at Yagel and consider how fragile she was, how available and simple her neck looked, how fatty her arms and how ample her thighs. She caught new angles when she saw her face in the mirror, a starkness that hadn't been there and now struck her as cunning. She went to the top of the stairs and stared

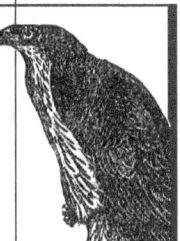

down them; she looked out the windows and her eyes caught the blur and skitter of countless beings, hiding behind and under things. She no longer cooked her food and finally Simyon coaxed her out with promises of meat, and locked the door against her.

SHE HAD SKIN stretched tight across the bones that pulled out from her shoulders, a hard elastic that wrinkled only when she pulled in her elbows firm against her ribs. When she stretched her arms out it was not possible to fight the tug, stronger than blood, that lifted her, or dropped her from great heights when she'd already been lifted. When she fell, it was with a liquid plummet, streamlined and terrible, her jaw slicing the air, her eyes tricking out every detail. Each movement in the air was adrenaline: she was pure and fast and vastly hungry. When she sighted her prey she started out silent and swift but just before she struck a large chaotic cry burst from her, turning the prey's eyes up, freezing their limbs. Just like that, food.

Small and furry; fat and hairy; clothed and crying; it didn't matter. The power was hers and in the air and right; what she could take was meant to be taken. High up, on the tips of the buildings, she could feel it all move beneath her, each little tiny patter, each needless drumming word. They soon took to rifles and guns and arrows, and she slipped behind buildings, faster than they were, and took them out when they pointed to where she'd been. As if she would ever stay where she once had been.

This was what she was meant to be and she filled her throat with the joy of it. ℮

Karen Heuler's story "Landscape, With Fish" appeared in the January/February 2008 issue of Weird Tales. She has published two novels and a short story collection, and has won an O. Henry award. Her latest novel, Journey to Bom Goody, concerns strange doings in the Amazon. She lives, writes and teaches in New York.

Right You Are IF YOU Say You Are

BY NORMAN SPINRAD

ILLUSTRATIONS BY MACSUGA

IN WHICH A MOST PERVERSE PRINCESS WANTS YOU TO SAVE HER ENTHUSIASTICALLY

Y OU ARE WALKING along a dirt road following a shallow stream burbling softly through a tunnel of over-arching tree-crowns, the loam under your feet dappled by the heavy shadow-dance of the branches and leaves, your nostrils riding high on the woodland aroma. Small birds sing and twitter. It's shady, but the air has the warmth of a summertime night. Though your feet do not exactly touch the ground, you're not floating, you're gliding, and you're doing it with effortless speed, glissing over the surface on the wings of the bird song.

There's no one else on this road but you, air-skiing down nature's Disneyland autobahn and towards the proverbial but now unwelcome light at the end of the tunnel. But when you pop out at the end of the arboreal birth canal, you find yourself in a mob scene.

You're smack-dab in a market outside a walled city. It's full of old women with wicker baskets squeezing the onions skeptically, country-weathered men in threadbare pantaloons and leather jerkins dipping wooden mugs into open beer-barrels, fly-specked sides of generic mammal displayed on trestles, roasting morsels of meat tended by small boys, dogs begging for scraps or stealing what they can and pissing where they want to, wooden carts bringing produce into the market from diverse somewheres, in the process of auctioning off their loads, being dragged towards the stone city walls by third-rate dray horses or second-rate donkeys. It smells of sweat, leather, beer, roasting meats, dung and piss, but the magic of the bright afternoon sun turns it into a happy enough perfume.

It would seem to be somewhen and where when knights were bold, for there's two of them in shining armor wending their way on horseback through the clamoring and odorous peasantry towards the open city gates. As if greeting their advent with proper fanfare, church bells within start pealing.

Sophisticated stuff. No unseemly and out-of-tune clanging or banging or bonging, but many many sets of mighty church-bell carillons playing in fugal harmony to turn Bach green with envy and not a discord or sour note.

You glide through the gates behind the knights, a discrete enough distance so that when one of their horses drops a load it doesn't land on you, and into downtown Medieval Wonderland.

Huge and hugely baroque churches everywhere — beautifully crafted monumental monuments of Gothic gingerbread stone and stained-glass glory singing their hearts out. Paving stone avenues between palaces and academies of alchemy. Squares with gargoyle fountains surrounded by ranks of taverns and restaurants. Venison, boar, chicken and duck on offer from open air barbecues. Food markets to be sure, but mar-

kets in jewelry, horses, clothing, and furniture, all of it of a proper civilized quality, at least as this upscale medieval tourist trap would have it.

There's obviously a great festival going on, for the streets of the city are *thronged* in a seemly manner, rather than anything so déclassé as *crowded*, with well-heeled pilgrims.

Knights in smartly-tailored steel suits, elegant ladies in veiled lace duncehats and yards and yards of gauzy gowns and trailing comets' tails of sandalwood and rose perfumes. Dukes and Duchesses by the dozens attended by happy peons, wizards and courtesans to the rich and famous or already rich and famous themselves. Monks and nuns from five-star monasteries and convents in their robe uniforms, bishops and even a cardinal or two in red cloaked plumage puttin' on the ritz.

Aside from these worthies themselves, no one is to be seen who is not catering to their trade or trying to, though without raucous hawking of the goods, which would only drive such aristocratic clientele away. Minstrels with lutes on every other corner with their peacock-plumed hats on the pavement to collect the coins. Any shop that can extending its display space out into the open air.

The genteel crowds seem to be spiraling slowly in towards some central attraction, and you float along with them on the florally-scented air, with the carillons brilliantly booming, and then, there you are.

This is not at all the geographical center of the city, but it certainly is the dramatic center. A great plaza has been built up against a section of the curving city wall, where it fences off a steep slope down to a rich green farmland plain below, a dramatic vista created when the peak of a small mountain was leveled to build the city.

Two incredible edifices bracket the plaza, facing each other across a large parkland space. Small copses of trees, beds of red and pink roses, neatly trimmed lawns are connected by a webwork of stone passage-

ways, along which well-groomed and -clad minstrels play, jongleurs juggle, sweets and wines and savory morsels are purveyed. What with the medieval gentry gamboling about, the sort of venue where it seems as if a unicorn might pop out of the shrubbery at any moment.

The eastward anchor of the gardens is the Cathedral, the crowning religious edifice of the city. A massive stone face festooned with saints and demons and gargoyles in Eden and points south, all painted in bright Disneyland colors, serves as no more than trelliswork for a huge stained glass rendition of Jesus Triumphant, His arms spread wide to form the cross and embrace the multitude taking their leisure below. On either side of this central figure, lesser cameos of lesser ecclesiastical lights. This stained glass façade is lit from within by so much torchlight that it glows like gently flickering neon. Twin carillons play in harmonious unison atop the tall bell towers, more stained glass in stonework trellises wind up around them, continuous spirals of a green-leafed vine that is also a serpent climb each of them to an image of the naked Adam atop the one and the naked Eve offering him an Apple on the other.

The Cathedral's rival for architectural *piece de resistance* of the city facing it across the plaza is an edifice only three stories in height but longer than the Cathedral is high, its walls of white marble encrusted with gilded brasswork twining about a vast scroll-like mural depicting noble jousts, gracious ladies in bulging bodice finery, knights on horseback slaying dragons and griffins and oversized serpents, unicorns in garden mazes, battles and seductions and musical performances, hunting parties and amorous interludes; all the figures life-size, a fairyland Middle Ages one might seemingly walk right into.

So you do.

You're in the rectangular inner courtyard of the building, a very formal garden, lawns you dare not set a sandal on, beds of brightly colored flowers arranged in decorous patterns. Lilac trees, rose bushes and well tended morning glory vines fill the air with drifting perfumes. Trees and gazebos, paths of polished pebbles, marble benches here and there, a fish pond, what seems like a swimming pool, thickets of marble cafe tables. Merles and canaries sing the only music, for the plebian entertainment of the city of church carillons staging their concert is prevented from disturbing these premises somehow.

Perhaps because it wouldn't dare.

People wander and saunter about, singly or in small groups, but within a space of this size they seem like the well-self-chosen few, with all the silk and velvet and lace, all the golden jewelry and gems, fancy swords and flamboyantly flowing superhero cloaks.

And those are only the men.

The women wear voluminous gowns with bursting bodices outlined in gold necklaces dripping diamonds and rubies, take-offs on knightly armor in leather and leopard skin, velvet pantaloons and peacock-plumed Robin Hood pillbox hats, capes which are the whole pelts of lions and tigers over skirted suits of brocaded silk, blouses and dresses of intricate hand-crocheted lace.

The courtyard is enclosed by three stories of porchways running all the way around each floor, a series of widely separated doors and large windows, some of them transparent glass and ironwork, some of them stained glass, some of them open to the balmy air, open out onto the walkways. Stairways connect them to each other and the ground. Like the outside of the building, it's all made of nothing less than marble, but there's no gilded gingerbread here, it's done in a sort of baroque Greek style, miniature columns embellished with miniature statues, all of it high-polished white.

For some perverse reason, the stairways to the first floor are at the corners, from there to the second is half a floor's walk away, back to the corners to the third, and then back to the middle to the top, a pointlessly overlong square spiral. But when you drift over to a staircase, you just start climbing, confident that you're going to enjoy every extra step of the way.

For every step of the way displays another masterpiece of the oil painter's art. They're in gilded frames and they're ensconced in stone niches all along the staircase walls, and when you emerge onto the first porch, you realize that there's no unused display space between doors and windows either.

The overall effect is richly pleasing in the manner of a brilliant patchwork quilt, for all the paintings are exactly the same size, about two feet square, as if they've all been commissioned by this establishment, whatever it is.

It must be some ultimately rich establishment because there are paintings by the thousands, and far from being hackwork or even merely competent, each and every one you pass is worthy of a master whose name would be respected in any century: landscapes, portraits, still-lifes, battle scenes, crucifixions, sumptuous nudes and nymphs, all beautifully rendered and glowing with thickly saturated color.

Servants in white gold-braided livery glide along the porches bearing trays of food and drink; pheasant embellished with its own plumage, wine in reddish crystal carafes with matching goblets, platters of meats and sweetmeats, miniature wooden beer kegs and tankards, elaborate gateaus. They're dancing in and out of the doors, and you gain glimpses of sumptuous apartments of diverse decor within, and you can see the scenes inside through as many of the windows as not.

Men and women accoutered as in the courtyard and with the same aristocratic insuisance recline upon couches before marble tables being served, in some apartments single musicians provide mood music on lutes or flutes or pipes, here and there you catch a stolen glance at a damsel in one degree of undress or another at her toilette, you hurry past a scene of intimate carnal passion.

A medieval version of the Louvre? Or a medieval Grand Hotel?

"Of course it's a *hotel*," says a querulous voice behind you. "You'd hardly call the Palace of the Virgin Princess an *inn*."

"Can you read my mind?" you exclaim as you whirl about.

"Of course I can read your mind — I'm a wizard, am I not? Whether there's anything in there worth reading remains to be seen."

Before you is a man in a black velvet pantalooned leisure suit sprinkled with stardust, and with a floppy black beret adorned with gold planetary broaches perched atop his long white hair. It's impossible to tell how old he is, a million years by the eyes, movie-star granddad by the rest of the face.

"You're Merlin the Magician?"

"*Merlin!* No, I am not Merlin and I am not a *magician!*"

He turns and is leading you impatiently up the stairway to the top floor. "I do not wow them around the Round Table with *magic tricks!* I'm a *wizard*, not a public personality, and no true wizard would be foolish enough to tell anyone his name, let alone have it broadcast by troubadours for the masses."

Having unburdened himself of his professional ire, the Wizard shrugs, laughs winningly.

"Sorry about that, but you will find that mention of that show-off's name to any true member of the guild will find you no favor."

"But this is a hotel?"

"This is not *a* hotel, this is *the* hotel, the grandest dame of a hotel for the grandest folk from all of Christendom, my man, gathering here for the annual great event."

"Great event — ?"

But you've reached the top floor and proceeded along a walkway to its midpoint, and there a medieval Tiffany glass window glowing from within suddenly opens up like a vertical clamshell revealing a breath-taking and blood-pounding vision of Venus.

She is naked, or rather, given the manner in which she displays what's on offer, classically nude.

"Who *is* she?"

What's on display is the body of a porn goddess, with perfected upturned-nipple breasts, athlete's body tone, and facial features of a twenty-five-plus-something wet-dream movie star, but displaying it hands on hips with the naked grace and fiery visage of a bored pirate challenging the world.

"Who is that? What is she *doing?*"

"That, of course, is the Virgin Princess of the Palace of the Virgin Princess, who else? And what she is doing is what she is doing every night, waiting for a knight to come and relieve her of the burning burden of her chastity, and that, of course, is going to be you."

"Me?"

"Who else, she's the Princess, I'm the Wizard, and you're the Hero of the tale."

"I am?"

"Of course this is your tale, but fear not, I am here to provide you with the necessary help."

"You will be my guide as Merl — "

"Don't mention that name! And no, I've got better things to do with my time than play nursemaid to some troubadour's hero, what you get from me is a single spell. That should be plenty, it's a very good spell indeed. Use it wisely."

The Wizard raises his arms, crosses his hands, and waves them about in a sardonic parody of a stage magician's act. "Abracadabra, eye of newt and snout of hog, and so on and so forth. Yes you are if you say you are. That's your spell. You're what you say you are. A duke, a cardinal, a scullery boy, rich man, poor man, beggarman, high-born thief."

He looks you up and down.

"You had better say you're a pre-paid guest in the hotel before someone summons the guards to throw you out, and you'd better look the part. Say it. You can even mumble it, no one has to hear it. Say *I am a paid-up guest in this hotel and I look like someone who belongs here.*"

"I am a paid-up guest in this hotel and I look like someone who belongs here."

And you do.

You are wearing flared velvet pantaloons in russet and burgundy panels, a matching puff-sleeved open tunic with white lace cuffs, a black cloak trimmed with gold brocade, a broad leather belt set with rubies and a massive gold buckle, a sword with a gilded silver grip in a chased silver scabbard, Puss in Boots footwear.

The Wizard prods you in the back with an elbow.

"She's been waiting for you for a long long time, Sir Hero, now get in there and strut your stuff. The rest is up to you."

And so you find yourself leaping through her boudoir window to confront a naked princess. You land on your feet in a large rose-colored room. The walls are essence of rose, the classy sassy tone between red and pink, the floors and ceiling are a deep rose red, and the abundance of gilt-framed mirrors are made of rose-tinted glass. White and yellow roses in gold vases are everywhere. Rosewood incense fogs the air.

The princess is looking you up and down, with a cool connoisseur's appraising eye that makes it hard to believe that this naked lady is a virgin, and the powerful rosewood musk she exudes doesn't do much for advertising her virginity either, nor does the huge canopied bed with its coverlet laid back rakishly to one side with refreshments arranged on the sideboards.

Upon completing her inspection, she shrugs. "All right, all right, at least you're here. Who are you?"

"I am a paid-up guest in this hotel. Don't I look like I belong here?"

"Everyone here had better be paid-up, and Saladin himself in his turban would look like he belonged here as long as he was. *Only* as long as he was. That's not what I was asking you. I was hoping you'd say you're a knight."

She's standing there utterly nude, displaying not only her perfect pulchritude, but displaying the attitude of anything but virgin innocence.

"You want me to be a knight?"

"There's a severe shortage of knights with the balls to leap through my window around here these dim days," she says contemptuously.

She backs up a few steps into the rosy world within in a manner that encourages you to follow. She spreads her raised arms upward, lifting her breasts even higher, forms a ballerina's arch, and pirouettes.

"I mean, look at this, if there is any such thing as a body to die for, am I not it? Is it not known far and wide that I have Christendom's largest collection of the erotic manuals of China and Inde and read them all so many times I know them by heart? The knight who liberates me from my virginity will receive the full carnal gratitude of a well-schooled expert, not the gawky naivete of a milk-maid in a haystack."

"If I told you I was a knight, and you believed me, what would you do?"

"I would do *everything* I've read about and waited to try for all these years," she breathes longingly.

"I am the knight who will liberate you from your virginity and you believe me, don't you?" you reply.

She looks you up and down somewhat differently. "I do believe I do," she says. "I do believe that you'll do." Then she turns on her heels offering you a beckoning finger over her shoulders as she sashays over to the bed.

She stretches herself out in an inviting recline, but when you reach the bed she springs up and glides into a full lotus of the sheets, touches your lips with a restraining forefinger.

"Not so fast, Sir Knight," she tells you. "Don't you know the ropes? The gallant who would free me to do what I most want to do in the world and get screwed deaf dumb and blind in the bargain has to slay the Dragon

and defeat the Black Knight in battle first. And believe me, I like the rules even less than you do! I thought you all knew that. I thought that's why a true knight for the night would never be mine. Those ball-less wonders!"

She unwinds from her lotus position and her arms are around your neck pulling you down into a long open-mouthed kiss.

"But I can see that *you're* not afraid of a little ol' lizard, now are you, hon'?" she breathes in your face with her hands on your thighs. "Just because no knight has yet slain the Dragon, doesn't mean it can't be done, I mean if any of them had, there wouldn't be a Dragon, now would there be, mon cher?"

"And how long has this been going on?"

The princess regards the ceiling, seems to be using her fingers and toes as an abacus, as she does some calculations in her head. "Five hundred and forty-three years, with a margin of error of three percent," she says blithely.

"And how many knights has the Dragon slain in five hundred and forty-three years?"

"Uh . . . " she mutters, "all of them."

"*How* many?"

"I don't know exactly, more than four hundred and less than five, I think," the princess admits blithely, as her hands begin to crawl up your thighs, "but half of them weren't even really knights. Back when this city was just a village, dozens of fools would give it a try when the Dragon appeared on the plain below each year on the day of its apparition, and that's a lot of the historical body-count. You didn't have to be a knight until the event became popular and a rich city's economy rose around it and knighthood was required to keep the riff-raff from providing low comedy instead of high mythic drama."

She sighs, she leans forward so that her nipples barely brush your chest with an electric tingle when she does. "But when the number of knights devoured by the Dragon became too well-known as the festival be-came famous, the supply of knights willing to take the beast on went south."

She rolls away onto the bed, and onto her back, with her hands behind her head proudly displaying her tantalizing loveliness, the body language of a blithe erotic invitation, but her face has a look of angry desperation.

"So generations did *this* to their princesses in order to keep the cowardly bastards coming, in order to keep the big show going, so that the city would continue to prosper off the tourist trade. The princess gets the hotel, so she's got an economic self-interest in keeping the Dragon alive, but unless some knight kills the thing, I am doomed to die a horny virgin like generations of my predecessors. How's *that* for a damned enchantment?"

She flips over onto her stomach and body-crawls towards you sinuously. "But it really doesn't matter, now does it?" she purrs. "If I lose either way, you could say I win either way, now couldn't you?"

She kisses you alternately up your left and right calves to your inner thighs. "Just between you and me, don't tell, but I've got enough squirreled away with some gnomes in the Alps to keep two people living in high style indefinitely. I'm well prepared to pay the consequences if you've got what it takes to slay my meal ticket. "

She produces a gauzy rose veil from a drawer, rubs it over her breasts and pubes, holds it up to you. "And this is my favor to crown your helm as you ride into battle to rid me of my horniness. I'm not rooting for my main attraction. What do you have to say to that, Sir Hero?"

"I say I am the knight in shining armor who will slay you your Dragon."

And you are. Or anyway you are indeed a knight in shining armor.

You are wearing a heavy steel suit and you peer through the eyeslit of a closed helmet. You're sitting on a horse likewise armored. You've got a sword in its scabbard buckled to your right side and a long lance in your left hand, a metal pole pointed with an outsized razor-sharpened steel arrowhead.

You're down there on the fruited plain as the last of a torrent of peasants evacuate themselves past you to join the thousands of them sitting on rude wooden stadium benches incised in the middle flank of the small mountain which is crowned by the city.

The lower few score yards of the slope are ominously empty of spectators save for six wizards, no doubt with sufficient spells to keep the Dragon from coming up after the customers. Above the bleacher seats, fancier and fancier grandstands rise class-wise to the feet of the city walls, stone benches, alcoves of stone with plush and leather cushions, alcoves with well-upholstered wooden furniture, private alcoves with velvet curtains being drawn back. Country hawkers ply the low-born with meat and bread and beer, and the quality of the stadium fare likewise rises toward the upper deck where it's piped in on silver platters by minstrels on flutes.

Atop the highest of high class pavilions perches what in Rome would be the Imperial Box at the Circus, a separate box done up like a little stage, floral vines gilding a white proscenium, red velvet drapes to the sides and atop framing twin thrones, one of silver and one of gold.

In the golden one sits the princess, naked as naked can be. Upon the silver throne sits what can only be the Black Knight, clothed as clothed can be, entirely enclosed in a suit and helmet of blackened steel, and with the visor down, so that not even his eyes can be seen.

The parapets of the city walls are crammed with a classless society of the more timid tourists except for the tops of opposing turrets where half a dozen wizards each hopefully guard the section of wall facing the plain.

Or do they?

The church carillons chime out a mighty orchestra of gravitas as the tower wizards raise their eyes and arms to the heavens, and the stained glass of the Cathedral win-

dows glow with an unearthly neon light, and a dark whirlwind thundercloud flashes into being above the plain.

They're not guarding the walls.

They're calling the Dragon.

"I am a knight in shining armor with a lethal lance and I am an expert swordfighter and horseman," you declare hopefully.

The thunderhead spreads out to blacken the sky and turn day into something like night over the now darkling plain to oohs and ahs from the hillside spectators behind you, but only for a moment. Then there is an immense explosion in the heavens that strobes a whited-out vision of the plain, with its huts and villages, its corrals and farm yards, its fields of grain and orchards of fruit, and then the vision vanishes as a rich sunset-colored mushroom pillar cloud forms out of the cloud-deck.

And out of it the Dragon arises in fire and brimstone to an ear-splitting peal of thunder in counterpoint to the church carillon orchestra.

A scaly green bat-winged pterodactyl bigger than a jumbo jet, with a long sinuous snaky tail ending in an ace-of-spades arrow-point soars up the mighty thermal of the dissipating mushroom pillar cloud, and as the sky returns to blue, it does a couple of loops, and a series of aerobatics that takes it to the far horizon, and then it power-dives from on high into a low glide towards you, its wings painting onrushing jagged shadows over the plain, its sonic boom flattening fields of crops, raking orchards of tree-crowns bare.

It alights on taloned feet about a football field's length downfield from you with a ballet dancer's grace. Now it's an enormous thunder-lizard, Godzilla out of Tyrannosaurus Rex, but it's so enormous that even from this far away, you can clearly see that it has a crocodile's head breathing fire and yellow fumes around a flickering serpent's tongue, that it has the compound insect eyes of twin military radar-domes done in black, that its wings have become a score or so of

writhing green tentacles thicker than fire hoses, each ending in the headless jaws of a tiger shark.

Even from this far away, the stink of fire and brimstone is almost overwhelming, and they can probably smell it all the way up to the city walls, choking sulfur fumes and tangy gunpowder burn, and riding beneath it, rotting meat in wet places, turtle tanks gone to thick algae, better you don't know.

This hideous and hideously lethal reeking monster does not lumber, but saunters agilely toward you to loud applause from behind you, and stops at midfield, where it goes through a series of instantaneous transformations while retaining its behemoth scale and its gunpowder, brimstone, and rotten slime body-odor.

An immense thing that might be a spider, if spiders had eighty legs instead of eight, tipped with hypodermic claws dripping venom, a razor-sharp beak lined with tiger's teeth, and were thirty yards tall.

Something like a glob of living Vaseline or an amoeba, larger than a whale, an otherwise featureless slime oozing along the ground, freckled and pocked and pimpled with hundreds of gnashing bear-trap mouths spitting napalm.

An immense mobile dung-pile with claws, and tentacles, and anal orifices clacking chitonous bills like the maracas of hell.

A pullulating mound of writhing white maggots, millions of little horrors adding up to a living communal organism even more ghastly than the sum of its parts.

All these and more, not quite rapidly enough to not be seen, but too rapid for the eye to really grab hold of, though the nose knows all too well on a deeply nauseating level that they're all somehow the same being.

The Dragon, something like the maggot pile only much more so, is the sum of many parts, is all of them and none of them, and is shuffling its avatars in front of you like a card-shark inviting a rube to play, strutting its demonic stuff.

This boastful display goes down well with the audience, after a fashion. There are boos and hisses from the grandstands, but they are well-mixed with cheers and applause; like a wrestling arena crowd, they can't root for the villain, but every show needs a villain you can love to hate, besides which it is, to say the least, quite a preliminary crowd pleaser.

"I am the knight who will slay you, Dragon," you declare, wondering if the spell can possibly work that far, "and I have a voice of thunder."

The first remains to be seen, but the latter seems to work as your next words roar into the Dragon's face as if through an amplifier and bank of stadium speakers. "I also have an impenetrable suit of light-weight Kevlar armor with Mylar insulation"

And you do. You're still a knight in still-shining armor, but the heavy steel armor has been replaced by a feather-light silvered suit and helmet that turns you into the Silver Surfer in his kendo practice gi.

The Dragon morphs into classic form. It's now standing on a pair of mighty but gracile legs like those of an ostrich, but green-scaled and with splayed multi-taloned feet, and it's about as tall as Godzilla, with huge leathery bat-wings casting a somber shadow of doom over you, with a head off a Tyrannosaurus Rex on steroids, a mouth full of silver teeth and red forked serpent's tongue, eye-holes that are black tunnels into deep pits where fires are burning far far away. It roars like a chorus of hoarse lions and spits a ball of flame that envelopes you in burning fire.

From which you emerge unconsumed and spreading your arms wide in silvery triumph to a great breath of awe from the crowd.

The horse you have been riding, however, has not been so lucky. Burned to a mouth-watering barbecue smelling turn, he's a rack of roast meat collapsing under you. The Dragon reaches down with clawed hands on the tips of its wings, snatches the roast horse out from under you, spilling you on the ground as it deposits it in its gaping maw, and chews it down with much cracking and slavering and smacking by the time you've gotten to your feet.

After which it leans down its long serpentine neck so that its awful rotten-egg reeking mouth and black pit eyes are right in your face. There are things moving around way down there in the darkness, things writhing in red torment, you can't make them out and you certainly don't want to join them, but the Dragon is clearly proclaiming that you are about to with its confident reptilian shit-eating grin.

The mouth widens, and widens, and widens, like that of a python preparing to swallow a goat whole, but displaying dentition that will allow it to chomp you down in marginally smaller chunks, and moves forward to envelope you.

"I am more than you can swallow, demon," you proclaim to the wide open spaces. "I am the Terminator."

The mouth becomes a roof above you as it descends, and the world entire as it closes on you, but you are the quickest of quicksilver, you ooze out through the teeth, reassemble human form, and take a bow to thunderous applause, like a matador whose cape has transfixed the bull.

The Dragon regards you with a certain lidded respect now perhaps. But there's something angry and enormous stirring down there at the bottom of those eyes of void, something red and fiery and fuming out sulfur. Crawling up towards you and coming ever closer.

Exploding up and out and around into a fiery wicker man huge as the Dragon had been, an enormous humanoid flame, its incandescent silhouette the body shape of a man with the feet of a lizard, the wings of bat, the neck of a brontosaur, and a head that might be human save for the horns above the sharp heavy brow, burning yet unconsumed like the Biblical Burning Bush but with a very bad attitude.

And from this fiery whirlwind a great and terrible voice doth speak, a voice like great rocks cracking under irresistible heat, like the roar of a furnace and the hiss of a concentration camp gas oven.

"I am come. Not my minions. I am come. I tire of this game. I am come to put an end to it. I am come to put an end to everything. I am come and this time I am come to stay. Glad to meet you, hope you guess my name."

The plain behind it splits in half as if this flaming demon were an anti-Moses parting not waters but dry land to reveal a fiery pit billowing choking radioactive yellow smoke and bubbling out all-consuming lava flowing slowly in all directions, including towards the crowd on the hillside and the city atop it.

It would seem that this apparition has never been part of the tourist attraction, is a lot more than anyone bargained for, as the crowd on the hillside grandstand scatters in all directions save toward the expanding lake of fire oozing up from the infernal depths. The wizards atop the wall towers who have unknowingly summoned His Satanic Majesty Himself now peer down fearfully from the parapets making furious passes with their hands that seem to accomplish nothing, while the mages supposedly guarding the lower slope of the hill abandon their posts at flank speed.

With every passing moment, it becomes clearer and clearer that the Dragon that has been devouring the flower of knighthood annually all these centuries in all its shapeshifting morphs has been the shadow-puppet show of the Prince of Liars, and now there are vague demonic forms coalescing and dissolving and coalescing again in the lava, like red hot molasses flowing down a creekbed.

And its equally clear that holding back the forces of Hell is entirely up to you.

"I am the knight come to slay you, and I have the power to command you to tell me how this may be done."

Sardonic laughter explodes from the flaming giant that shakes the heavens and rumbles the earth. "You cannot slay me," says that immense and immensely reptilian voice. "But you might slay this Dragon."

And in an eyeblink it is a Dragon towering before you, its feet placidly planted in the burning lava, a huge scaly saurian with the night-thing wings of a giant vampire bat and a neck like the body of a python. But the head on that slowly curling and uncurling neck is that of a man.

Well, not exactly.

It has the general shape of a human head except for the small horns growing out from above prominent brows as sharp as scimitars, and its mouth and the sardonic smile there are entirely human, but its ears are large and pointed and mobile, and its complexion is fire-engine red.

But the least human aspect of this demonic visage is the eyes, the black pits of non-being, of void, more terrible still than before with what had lurked there now emptied out into the world as the neck of the Dragon curls down to confront you at close quarters with its grinning demonic face.

"I can only be prevented from working my will and making the world my own," he tells you in a soft serpent's voice that only you can hear. "My Dragons can be slain. You may notice that the world does not abound in them." He laughs. "But you may also notice that noble knights in shining armor are an equally endangered species. And if the Last Dragon slays the Last Knight I will end my lonely exile in the flaming pit and be released at last upon the world."

"But if the Last Knight slays the Last Dragon?"

"The world will never know what it has been saved from. But he will know. As you now know. And perhaps they will be one and the same. Every knight who has tried to slay this Dragon has fought in the faith that it might be the last one. For who knows but me, he might be. You might be."

Again that sarcastic laugh right in your face.

"But of course this Dragon slew them all. It too has fought as if it were the last of its kind. For a thousand years. Those are the *rules* of my game. And if you should win it, without a Dragon to open it, this gateway will be closed. That is the *nature* of my game."

"I am the man who will kill this Dragon," you declare, hoping your single spell will hold.

"Are you now?"

"I have the power to command you to reveal to me how it may be done."

"Do you now?"

"Yes."

The strangest expression warps that satanic visage even further. Shock? Surprise? Rage? Amusement? Somehow it seems to be all of them.

"I do believe you do," it hisses with much the same unreadable bad attitude, and manages to shrug the coils of its sinuous neck. "It might even improve my game. It has become boringly predictable for the last millenium or so."

Another sulphurous laugh right in your face.

"Only a Dragon can slay this Dragon."

The loudest, most sardonic, and hot wet laugh of all in your face, no doubt intended to be the last. "So the only way you can kill this Dragon is to persuade this Dragon to kill itself."

And the Dragon reels in its serpentine neck, spreads its leathery wings, and springs up out of the lake of lava into the air, climbs to a hundred meters or so, flies a lazy circle, and comes back and down at you shouting "And I don't think this Dragon is going to do that? Do you?"

"I am Godzilla, I am Tyrannosaurus Maximus, I am the Heavyweight Champion Dragon of the World, and a Black Belt in Street Fighting too!" you roar back.

And you are.

The previously fearsome Dragon making its death swoop towards you becomes

something you swat out of the air with one clawed fist like King Kong swatting an unfortunate biplane atop the Empire State Building. You catch it with your other great claw before it can fall into the lake of fire in which you stand, and which means nothing to you. You hold it up before you by the edges of its wings, crucifying it in mid-air.

"I am become a Dragon to slay the Dragon!" you roar on a wind of flame. And you grab it round its scrawny neck like a chicken and hold its little face up to your immense iron-jawed mouth.

"And therefore the Dragon you slay cannot be the last," the head laughs as you bite it off the Dragon's neck. "And you cannot be the noble knight who slew it, now can you Sir Hero?" the severed head continues to taunt you even as you spit it out. "And so, if not here, I will return somewhere and the game goes ever on."

The lake of fire is suddenly gone. The fiery gash in the body of the earth is healed without a scar as if it has never been. The corpse of a giant winged lizard with a lance through its heart is gathering the attention of the vultures and crows.

You are wearing a suit of steel armor gleamingly with shining silver plating. The visor of your helmet to match is open to the sweet smell of righteous victory and after a long uncertain gaspy silence, your ears inside it echo with the music of thunderous applause and joyous church-bells.

You turn to regards the hillside grandstands, now filled with orderly ranks of applauding spectators, once again neatly assorted by class, and you take your bow.

The theatrical private box atop the most luxurious level of pavilions is empty however. Neither the Princess nor the Black Knight has stuck around to pay you homage. But then a wizard commands a previously invisible door in the wall separating the hillside stands from the plain of battle.

And out strides not the naked Virgin Princess but the Black Knight.

He strides up to you like some sort of perfected robotic Darth Vader. Completely enclosed in finely articulated black armor. Faceless behind the black helmet's mask whose only features are a pair of nostril holes, a thin lipless slit for a mouth, and the hint of an abstract browridge shadowing a smaller slit for each eye.

"You have slain the Dragon, and gained the right to deflower the Virgin Princess, who is thinking of naught but her own erotic satisfaction at last, but first you must get through the Black Knight, who is not wriggling in horny anticipation."

The voice that issues from those immobile metal lips is not robotic by any means, it is all too human in its anger, but the tonalities of it have been flattened and coldened to metal as if by a vocoder.

"And I am not at all pleased," the Black Knight tells you, as if you couldn't already guess. "And neither will the denizens of my city be when the applause dies down and the tourist trade does a slow slide into the jakes. Eros might be pleased for a night that you slew our Dragon, but Mammon wakes up in the morning when she remembers that it was her Dragon too that you slew, and her hotel business with it."

The Black Knight whips off one steel glove with the other and slaps you gently across the face with it. "The Black Knight challenges you to a duel to the death, Sir Hero of Eros and Villain of Mammon, you don't get anywhere near her, except by getting through me."

"The Black Knight's on to you, my Hero," says the voice of the Princess behind you.

You turn, and as you do, you are no longer on the battle plain, you are in the boudoir of the Virgin Princess, and your prize is stretched out longingly naked and spread-eagled on her bed with a long contract scroll draped like a flag over her most private parts.

"Believe me I like this less than you do, hon," she tells you, pointing a finger at a locus on the scroll, "but it says so right here, the victorious knight must best the Black Knight in unarmed free form wrestling."

"I have no problem with that," you say, "I have a black belt in every martial art on Earth."

"I'm afraid you don't this time, hon," the Princess croons. "Sez right here in the rules, no biting, no blows to the crotch . . . and no magic spells."

"And those are the *only* rules," says the Black Knight. "We fight each other until one of us gives up or dies."

When you turn this time, you are no longer in the boudoir of the Princess, you're standing on the canvas of a wrestling ring pinned in bright yellowish white light so that nothing can be seen beyond the ropes as if there is nothing there but the void. No spectators, no referee, just you and the Black Knight, together and alone in the ring.

Now the Black Knight has shed metal armor for a black karate suit and black fencer's helmet that reveal nothing more than before. But you reveal almost everything, naked save for a silvery bikini jockstrap suitable for Muscle Beach and a gauzy standard of rosy cloth tucked into it.

What is revealed is a body that would stand out from the gym rats anywhere, as if the Princess has slipped you one more minor spell under *wish fulfillments, clause four b paragraph 2a.*

Thus emboldened, you bow lightly and very briefly, the Black Knight does likewise, and you are upon each other.

You reach out to conquer the Black Knight with the sheer might of your irresistible bear-hug, but the Black Knight summersaults forward, and rolls out with a kick that just misses your head as you duck under it, drop to the canvas, and roll like a barrel into the legs of the Black Knight, bringing your opponent tumbling down over your back.

But tumbling down in good order, for the Black Knight rolls once, twice, thrice, across the ring while you're bouncing up again, and rockets off the ropes with an open-legged forward dive rather than a kick which clamps your waist in strong muscular thighs, and rolls you over into a take-down.

You're on your back with the Black Knight astride you, forelegs crossed under you, thighs gripping you, leaning over your face with that blank unreadable mask. But your arms are free, your back is strong, and you raise your torso upwards with lower back muscles alone like a cobra, hands reaching out to grab your opponent by the throat.

The Black Knight then has no problem grabbing *you* by the throat, and there you squat in a most peculiar sort of lotus position, with you and the Black Knight face to face in extreme close-up holding each other by the throat, your upper torso held upright by the force in your pelvic chakra, as it were, but the lower body that contains it pinned to the mat.

"This would appear to be a checkmated position," the voice of the Black Knight says, "I don't think it's in the Olympic wrestling manual, and there's no referee."

Is there something different about that voice? Certainly the lighting is different, unshadowed or shaded, but a rosy red now, a rose red floodlight on a wrestling mat turned satin rose colored sheets.

"One of us is going to have to give up or we'll be here like this forever," you declare.

"Let us simply wrestle it to one fall," replies the Black Knight. "Whoever pins the other to the mat gets to work their will."

It's definitely the voice of the Princess now, though the electronic cutting edge of the Black Knight is still there too. "I warn you, the Black Knight is not rolled over easily. This is the real thing, this is not show business."

You feel the Black Knight's hands tightening around your throat. You tighten yours. Using all the strength of your back, you try to pry yourself free from the grip of Black Knight's thighs.

There's something different about the thighs wrapped over your pelvis now, no lessening of strength, yet a kind of softening, and there's the fragrant smell of rose perfume in the air. It's coming from the black mask breathing it in your face as she speaks.

"This isn't in the Kama Sutra either, is it, hon?"

"Neither is this, and it probably isn't in the Marquise de Queensbury either, but maybe you won't really mind," you say as you suddenly roll sideways, turning the tables as you release your hands from the Black Knight's throat, rip off the black hood, and come up atop the Princess kissing her rose-red lips, inhaling the perfume of her avid hot breath, as the Black Knight suit does a dissolving striptease.

She leans back in a nest of pillows and opens her arms to you and her legs delightedly and delightfully akimbo.

"Any knight in shining armor might rescue a Virgin Princess from her Dragon, hon," she purrs, "but you gotta be something special to rescue her from her Black Knight. Maybe that spell is still working? At least we can give it the old college try."

"I am your tireless perfect lover," you tell her, "and tonight's your night to howl!" you declare as you glide atop her perfect body saying the magic words. ◉

Norman Spinrad *is the author of more than 20 novels and 60 or so short stories, feature film scripts, TV scripts, songs, and much assorted other stuff. He is a former president of the Science Fiction and Fantasy Writers of America and World SF. He is currently working on co-producing a film of his novella* Vampire Junkies *and writing a novel called* Welcome To Your Dreamtime, *from which this story is taken.*

SUMMER READING WEIRDUCOPIA

*Vacation season is here ~ and that means
it's time to turn off the TV, log off the Internet,
and pick up a book! Here's an eclectic look
at some fun recent releases ~ starting with
an exclusive sneak peak at the hot new
steampunk epic from Tor Books . . .*

The Court of the Air

CHAPTER I

BY STEPHEN HUNT

Molly Templar sat dejected by the loading platform of the Handsome Lane laundry. An empty cart bore testament to the full tub of clothes inside, bubbling away. At least Molly tried to imagine what dejected would feel like, and scrunched her freckled face to match the mood. In the end, though, it was one of the other poorhouse girls, Rachael, who came to fetch her, not the Beadle, so Molly's player-like mastery of 'dejected' went unappreciated.

Damson Snell, the mistress of the laundry, came out to see who had turned up, and looked disappointed that it was just another Sun Gate workhouse girl. 'The Beadle too busy to see the quality of the idle scruffs he's forcing on my business, then?'

'His apologies, miss,' said Rachael. 'He is otherwise engaged.'

'Well, you tell him from me, I got no room for workers as slack as this one.' Snell pointed to Molly. 'You know what I caught her doing?'

'No, miss.' Although Rachael's tone suggested she might have an inkling.

'Reading!' Damson Snell's face went red with incredulity. 'Some gent had left a thruppence novel in the pocket of his coat and she —' her finger stabbed at Molly '— was only bloody reading it. And when I bangs her one, she cheeks me back. A fine little madam and no mistake. You tell the Beadle we runs a place of work here, not a library. When we wants a lady of letters, I'll send for an articled clerk, not some Sun Gate scruff.'

Rachael nodded with her best impression of contrite understanding and led Molly away before the laundry owner could extend her tirade.

'A fine lesson in business from her,' said Molly, when they were out of earshot. 'She who slips the Beadle twenty shillings a month and gets her labour free from the poorhouse. Her lesson in economics forgot to include a fair wage for those who have nothing to sell but their labour.'

Rachael sighed. 'You're turning into a right little Carlist, Molly. I'm surprised you weren't turned out for trying to organize a worker's combination. That thruppence novel in the gent's pocket wasn't a copy of *Community and the Commons*, was it?'

'From one of her customers?' Molly snorted. 'No, it was a naval tale. The jolly aerostat *Affray* and its hunt for the submarine pirate Samson Dark.'

Rachael nodded. The Kingdom of Jackals was awash with writers from the publishing concerns along Dock Yard, sniffing out heroes, bandits, highwaymen and privateers to fill the pages of pocket news sheets like *The Middlesteel Illustrated News* and the cheap penny dreadfuls, fact and fiction blended into cut-price serials to hook the readers. The more imaginative stories even plundered legend, culling gods from the dark days before the citizens of Jackals embraced the Circlist meditations; writing devils like the wolftakers onto the pages of their tales, fiends sent to kidnap the wicked and terrify the immoral with their black cloaks and sharp teeth.

Viewed from the workhouse, the stories were bright distractions, an impossible distance from the children's lives of grind and hunger. Molly wanted those stories to be true, that if only somewhere there might be bright ballrooms and handsome officers on prancing horses. But the hard-bitten streak of realism in her realized that Samson Dark had probably been a violent old soak, with a murderous temper and a taste for cargoes he was too lazy, idle and stupid to earn himself. Far from fighting a glorious battle, the jolly airship *Affray* had probably blundered across the pirate fleet feeding innocent sailors to the fish, then held position over Dark's underwater vessel while they tumbled fire-fins into her masts and deck, leaving the burning pirates to the mercy of the ocean and the slipsharps. Days later some hack from Dock Yard would have chanced across the drunken aerostat crew in a tavern, and for the price of a keg of blackstrap, teased out an embellished tale of glory and hand-to-hand combat. Then the hack would have further embroidered the yarn for his editors on the penny dreadfuls and Dock Street imprints like the Torley Smith Press.

Hardcover ~ $25.95 ~ Tor Books
In stores now

'Have I been blown to the Beadle yet?' asked Molly, her concerns returning to the present.

'As if you wouldn't have been,' said Rachael. 'Though not by me — I'm no blower. This is the fourth job you've been chucked from in as many months. He was going to find out somehow.'

Molly teased her red hair nervously. 'Was the Beadle angry?'

'That's one word for it.'

'Well, what can he do?' asked Molly.

'You're a fool, Molly Templar,' said her companion, seeing the flash of defiance in Molly's eyes. 'What haven't they done to you? The strap? Administrative punishment, more days on than off? Short rations? And still you ask for more.'

'I'm out of it soon enough.'

'You've still got a year to go before your ward papers expire and you get the vote,' said Rachael. 'That's a long time to have the Beadle pissed off at you.'

'One more year, then I'm out of here.'

'To what?' asked Rachael. 'You think an orphan scruff like you or me is going to end up nobbing it up in grand society? Being waited on with partridge pie and the finest claret? You don't settle to a living soon and you'll end up running with the flash mob on the street, dipping wallets, then the crushers will have you and it'll be a transportation hulk to the Concorzian colonies for our young Damson Molly Templar.'

CLOCKWORK HEART
by Dru Pagliassotti
(Juno Books, $6.99)

Flight goggles on her face, a winged apparatus strapped to her back with leather and buckles, Taya makes the picture-perfect steampunk heroine: an icarus, a working-class courier who flies above the city of Ondinium, carrying messages to society's masked elite. Pagliassotti's clockwork world is driven by punch cards running on a colossal-geared computational engine, and her story is fueled by the triangle of intrigue between Taya, a charismatic nobleman, and his surly geek brother.

HOLLOW EARTH
by David Standish
(Da Capo Press, $16.95)

With a subtitle like "The Long and Curious History of Imagining Strange Lands, Fantastical Creatures, Advanced Civilizations, and Marvelous Machines Below the Earth's Surface," David Standish pretty much lays out right there on the cover what kind of treat the reader is in for. The author does a masterful job of tracing the way a single, far-out idea connects countless people and things across history, from Halley's Comet to Uncle Wiggily.

'I don't want to end up back there.' Molly flipped a thumb in the direction of the Handsome Lane laundry.

'Nobody wants to end up there, Molly girl. But if it puts food in your tummy and a roof over your head, it's better than starving.'

'Well, I'm being starved by a gradual process in the poorhouse, or by a quick one out of it,' said Molly. 'If only . . .'

Rachael took Molly's hand. 'I know. I miss the damson too. And if wishes were shillings we'd all be living like princesses.'

There was only one damson for the orphans. Damson Darnay had been the head of the Sun Gate poorhouse before the Beadle; four years now since her heart attack. A reformer, she had argued that the rich financial district of Middlesteel could afford a model poorhouse on its doorstep. A house where the children were taught to read and write, where the mindless make-work of the poorhouse was replaced by an education and a good Circlist upbringing.

It was a vicar from the Circlean church who had taken away her shroud-wrapped body on the back of a wagon one cold morning, and the Beadle who turned up to take her place. In the pocket of the local merchants, the cost of their keep was now defrayed by placement in local businesses. Ward apprenticeships to prepare the grateful orphans for their necessary adult living.

It was strange how the children's placements never included perching behind a warm desk in one of the fancy new pneumatic buildings along Gate Street, or an articled clerk's position along Sun Lane. Sewer-scrapers, yes. Laundry jobs that would see your nails fall out from constant dipping in chemical bleach. Positions in dimly lit workshops and mill works, hunched over a loom or cutting engine, splashed by metal and losing a finger a year.

Small for her age, Molly had spent her own twelfth and thirteenth years as a vent girl, climbing the dark airshafts of the Middlesteel pneumatics with a brush, unclogging the dust and stack smoke. That was before the Blimber Watts tower breach. Fifty storeys high, Blimber Watts had been a pioneering design for its time, able to house thousands of clerks, marble atriums and even a sun garden inside its rubberized and canvas skin. But the draughtsmen had got the stress calculations wrong and the water walls had burst, sending the pneumatic structure tumbling down into the clogged streets.

Molly had been in the vents on the thirty-eighth floor when the tower lost cohesion, coming down even faster than it had gone up. Clawing in darkness at the deflating walls as her stomach turned in freefall; a smashing impact, then lying trapped for five days between two leaking water cells, licking at the walls for the stale, dirty liquid. Throwing up in terror, her voice a knife-slicing croak screaming and screaming for help.

She had lost hope of being rescued, lying in the embrace of a pressing crush of rubber. Then she sensed the steamman worker cutting through the building's remains above her. Molly knew she possessed an unnatural affinity for the mechanical race, the polished boiler hearts and intricate mechanisms of cogs and silicate prisms calling out to her to be examined, turned over in her fingers, assembled into intricate patterns. She had screwed her eyes shut and willed the worker to hear her thoughts — here, here, down HERE.

Minutes later the silent steamman had peeled back a foot-thick strip of rubber, letting a flood of impossibly bright daylight come gushing in. It stood there silently, an iron statue, until Molly noticed its voicebox had been removed. A gentle nod of its head and the steamman was moving off, as if bloodied, blackened girls crawling out of the ground were an everyday occurrence for the creature of the metal.

How the Beadle had cursed and beaten her to try to get her back into the vents. But the only time she had tried, two other vent girls had to be sent in to drag her trembling, mute form out of the passages.

'Come on,' said Rachael. 'Let's take the turn down Blackglass Lane; they were putting on a march across Grumblebank when I came to fetch you.'

'The King?' said Molly.

'Better than that, girl. The Special Guard.'

Despite the trouble that was waiting for her back at the workhouse for another job lost, Molly smiled. Everyone loved the Special Guard. Their extreme powers. The handsome cut of their uniform. Days spent at the muscle pits to whet the curves of their athletic build.

The two girls cut across a series of old rookeries, bent and puddled with garbage filth, before emerging on one of the broad clean avenues that ran parallel to Sun Street itself. There, a crowd of eager onlookers were thronging the street, a line of crushers from the local police precinct holding the press back, dark bandoleers of gleaming crystal bullets crisscrossed over their black constable's uniforms.

Back down the thoroughfare a column of the Special Guard moved with their trademark sweeping leg march, high boots whip-cracking on the road in unison. The ground seemed to vibrate with their approach.

'There's your guardsmen,' said Molly.

'And there's your king,' added Rachael.

His Majesty King Julius, eighth monarch of the Throne Restored and King of the Jackelians, sat on a cushioned red seat in an open coach and four, staring sadly back at the curious crowds.

Molly gestured at Crown Prince Alpheus sitting to the king's side, hardly any older than either of the poorhouse girls. 'He doesn't look happy.'

'Why should he be, when his father's got the waterman's sickness? His pappy won't see out another two years as monarch, then the boy's for the knife.'

Molly nodded. The King's robes had been subtly tailored to accentuate the fact that both of his arms had been surgically removed, and in time the young prince would no doubt be dragged bawling to the bonecutter's table by his Special Guard jailers.

It had been ever thus, since Isambard Kirkhill strode across the land in a sea of blood and pistol smoke to assert parliament's right of supremacy at the head of the new pattern army. No monarch shall ever raise his arms against his people again.

Five hundred years since the civil war and the House of Guardians were still adhering to the strictures of Isambard Kirkhill, 'Old Sabreside' as his enemies had nicknamed him. There was the weekly march

DOGS by Nancy Kress
(Tachyon Publications, $14.95)

So has enough time passed that you've forgotten all about the hypothetical threat of the avian flu epidemic? Well, guess what: it's time for the dog flu. In Nebula and Hugo Award-winning author Nancy Kress's dark new thriller, vicious bio-zombie dogs begin slaughtering their owners. Is this mutant virus merely an ugly new form of 21st-century terrorism, or something more sinister still?

TIGERHEART by Peter David
(Del Rey Boks, $22)

Peter David first became known for his fresh, charming takes on iconic characters — the Hulk, the crew of the *Enterprise* — before going bestseller in his own right with the sarcastic fantasy hero Sir Apropos of Nothing. David's return to the mass-cultural toybox is a triumph: *Tigerheart* does for Peter Pan what *Wicked* did for Oz's Witch of the West, taking dear friends from childhood fantasy and shining the spotlight on them from unexpected new directions. Meet the new Boy Who Wouldn't Grow Up . . .

BEST OF THE BUBBAS OF THE APOCALYPSE by Selina Rosen
(BenBella Books, $14.95)

Bruce Campbell has played Elvis, and Bruce Campbell has played opposite zombies, and Bruce Campbell is awesome, right? So imagine *how awesome* a book full of stories about good ol' boys facing off against zombies in a world where Elvis is god would be! No, Campbell has nothing to actually do with it, beyond the subtext, but come on: "Zombie Fu." "It Came From Willy McCracken's Buttocks." "Iron Chef Bubba: Battle Possum." AWESOME.

THE EXECUTION CHANNEL
by Ken MacLeod
(Tor Books, $14.95)

Any run-of-the-mill conspiracy theorist can imagine a world where the U.S. government secretly plotted 9/11. Ken MacLeod gives us a creepy global twilight zone where the nuking of Scotland is only the key to a bigger puzzle; a mysterious "Execution Channel" broadcasts killings 24/7 while bloggers lament that it doesn't show "spammers being beaten to death with baseball bats"; and an unexpected revelation jolts us into realizing just how depressingly familiar alternate realities could be.

to Parliament Square from the palace — the latter little more than an empty marble jail now. The symbolic unchaining of the king's iron face-gag, then the king would bend down on one knee and assert the House of Guardians' right to rule for the people. These days his only witnesses were a few uninterested spectators, a handful of curious foreign visitors and the long line of silent statues of Guardian Electors past.

'Look,' said Molly, pointing behind the carriage. 'Captain Flare.'

Rachael pushed at the costermongers and fish-stall hawkers in front of her to get a better look. 'It is him. Molly, will you look at those muscles? He could crush a regiment of Cassarabian sand riders between them thighs.'

Molly knew that Rachael favoured the lewder penny dreadfuls, adventures that featured the action between the silks of dune-swept harems as much as the ring of sabre steel across a battlefield. But it was true. The commander of the Special Guard was impossibly handsome. None of the penny dreadfuls' cover illustrations had ever done him justice. Captain Flare's cloak drifted behind him like a thing alive, a dancing shadow, his piercing blue eyes sweeping the crowd, making them feel he was staring straight at each of them alone. A flash of light glinted off the captain's restraining neck torc, blinding Molly for a second.

'Hooray the Guard!' An almost hysterical scream from one of the crowd, and as if it were a trigger, the entire multitude took up the shout, cheering and stamping along the broadways. Someone in the crowd started singing 'Lion of Jackals' and soon half the avenue had joined in the bawdy patriotic lyrics.

Molly stood next to Rachael, cheering, a swell of pride rising in her chest. Hooray the Guard indeed. Between the Royal Aerostatical Navy ruling the sky and the powerful and heroic Special Guard on the ground, demolishing any enemy that dared to threaten Jackals, the kingdom was the most powerful force on the continent.

Other nations would have used that power to build an empire, bully their neighbours into subservience. But not Jackals. Their people suffered no rule of mad kings, powerhungry caliphs or rapacious senators. The quiet, peaceful Jackelians had pulled the teeth of their own would-be overlords and had prospered for centuries — trading, building, and quietly, doggedly innovating. If a Jackelian had a town garden to potter around in, or a village field to snatch a quick afternoon game of four-poles in, their empire was complete.

Other nations had dictator kings, political assassinations, and the heart-tugging wail of starving children and barren fields lying fallow while peasant armies slaughtered each other at the whim of local warlords. Jackals let its over-ambitious fools argue and wag fingers at each other across the House of Guardians.

Other nations had dark gods and wild-eyed prophets that demanded obedience, child mutilation, slavery, and poverty for the people while wealth flowed to an all-powerful priest class. Jackals had its deity-free Circlist philosophy, gentle meditations and a wide network of oratories. A Circlist parson might drop round and request a quick brew of caffeel, but never call for the beating heart of a family's firstborn to be ripped out of its chest.

Every few decades a foreign power would mistake the Jackelians' quiet taste for the rule of law for the absence of ambition. Would mistake a content and isolationist bent for a weak and decadent society. Would come to the conclusion that a nation of shopkeepers might better be put to serving what they had built, made and grown to warriors and bullies. Many enemies had made the assumption that *prefers not to fight* equates to *can't fight* and *won't fight.* All had been punished severely for it. Slow to rouse, once they were, their foes discovered Jackals was no nation full of bumbling storekeepers, greedy mill owners and stupid farm boys. They found a pit of lions, a people with a hard, unruly thuggish streak and no tolerance for bullies — either foreign or raised on Jackals' own acres. Of course, being the only nation on Earth to possess a supply of celgas had never harmed the kingdom's standing. Jackals' unique aerial navy was truly the envy of the world, a floating wall of death standing ready to guarantee her ancient freedoms.

'Better a knave in Jackals than a prince in Quatérshift' went the popular drinking song, and right now, caught up in the wild jingoistic crowd, Molly's heart followed the sentiment. Then she remembered the Beadle waiting for her back at the poorhouse with his stinging cane and her heart briefly sank. Her spirit quickly returned; she found her resolve stiffened as she remembered one of Damson Darnay's history lessons. Each of them was a gem to be treasured in her now miserable life, but one in particular she recalled with fond clarity, even now, years after the death of the woman who had been like a mother to her.

The lesson had taken the form of a centuries-old letter — a horrified report to the then King of Quatérshift from his ambassador in Jackals, generations before Jackals' civil war, when most of the continent still suffered under the heel of absolutist regimes. The monarch of the old throne of Jackals had been attending a play at the theatre when the mob took against the performance, booing the actors off the stage, then, noticing the King in the royal box, stoning him too.

The stunned Quatérshiftian had described to his own monarch the unbelievable sight of the King's militia fighting a rearguard action down the street as the rioting mob chased the portly Jackelian ruler away from the burning theatre. How alien to that bewildered ambassador, from a land where compliant serfs would be beaten to death for failing to address a noble with respect. But how true to the Jackelian character.

Molly had taken that lesson to heart. She might be an orphan, brought up by an uncaring state, but she would brook no bullying, and she was equal in the eyes of the law to any poorhouse official or Middlesteel laundry owner. Now, if only the Beadle could see things that way.

T HE HEAD OF the Sun Gate workhouse had an office increasingly at odds with the rest of the poorhouse's shabby buildings, from his shining teak writing desk, through to the rich carpets and the obligatory oil painting of the current First Guardian, Hoggstone, hung behind it all. After Molly realized the Beadle did not seem inclined immediately to start screaming a tirade of abuse at her, the second thing she noticed was the calm presence of the elegant lady seated on

LOVE + SEX WITH ROBOTS
by David Levy (Harper, $24.95)
We've all seen the imagery inching closer to reality: Jude Law as a pleasure droid in *AI.* The sexbot dispensing booze from her innards in that vodka commercial. The alarmingly realistic, lifesized RealDolls that Howard Stern infamously called "better than a real woman." Artificial intelligence expert David Levy takes a fascinating look at the weird phenomenon of how people are ever more conditioned to form emotional attachments to artificial representations of life — even to the point of choosing invented love over the messiness of the real thing.

THE CALL OF THE WEIRD
by Louis Theroux
(Da Capo Press, $15.95)
A decade ago, Louis Theroux hosted a British documentary on bizarre U.S. subcultures. Now, in *The Call of the Weird,* he goes back to see how his subjects are faring, introducing us to a spectrum of anomalous Americans ranging from Heaven's Gate cult survivors to UFO true-believers. Theroux shows an uncanny ability to paint these so-called weirdos in all their gloriously intimate humanity.

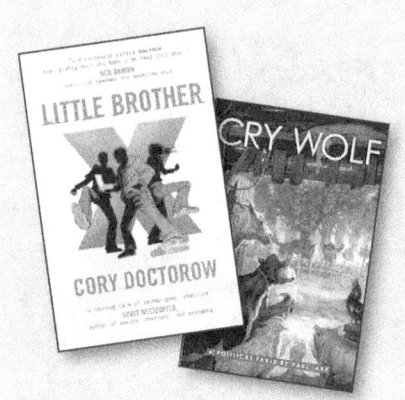

LITTLE BROTHER
by Cory Doctorow
(Tor Books, $17.95)

Author Cory Doctorow was just a kid when he started living an activist life, fighting the proverbial Man alongside the likes of Greenpeace; ever since, he's been weaving near-future narratives, both fictional and not, infused with a strong social consciousness. With *Little Brother* he's given us a novel for the era: In the aftermath of a catastrophic terrorist attack on San Francisco, an innocent, too-smart 17-year-old whose online handle is "w1n5t0n" gets swept up in Homeland Security's net — and soon finds himself the reluctant poster boy for an underground movement to jam the government's abuses of power.

CRY WOLF by Paul Lake
(BenBella Books, $12.95)

Also finding inspiration in Orwellian dystopias is Paul Lake, who uses the talking-critters model of *Animal Farm* to give us a right-wing perspective (a *goose's* right wing, that is) on today's illegal-immigrant debate. When a group of civilized barnyard animals allow an injured wild doe to take shelter on their farm, it's the first tumble down a slippery slope that ends in a full-fledged takeover by hordes of rapacious beasts from the wilderness.

his chaise longue. Smart. Quality. Too richly dressed for any inspector of schools. Molly eyed the Beadle suspiciously.

'Now, Molly,' began the Beadle, his lazy con-man's eyes blinking. 'Sit down here and I will introduce you to our guest.'

Molly prepared her best barrack-room lawyer's face. 'Yes, sir.'

'Molly, this is Damson Emma Fairborn, one of Sun Gate's most prominent employers.'

The lady smiled at Molly, pushing back at the curl of her blonde bob, streaked by age with a spray of platinum silver now. 'Hello, Molly. And do you have a last name?'

'Templar,' said the Beadle, 'for the —'

The lady crooked a finger in what might have been displeasure and amazingly the Beadle fell silent. 'Molly, I am sure you can speak for yourself . . .'

'For the Lump Street temple, where the Aldermen found me abandoned, wrapped in a silk swaddle,' Molly said.

'Silk?' smiled Damson Fairborn. 'Your mother must have been a lady of some standing to have thrown good silk away. A dalliance with the downstairs staff, or perhaps an affair?'

Molly grimaced.

'But of course, I am sure you have dwelt on the identity of your parents at some length. There is not much else to occupy the mind in a place like this, after all.'

A sudden shocking thought gripped Molly, but the lady shook her head. 'No, Molly. I am not she; although I suppose I am of an age where you could be my daughter.'

The Beadle harrumphed. 'I should warn you, Molly has something of a temper, damson. Or should I say temperament.'

'To match her wild red hair, perhaps?' smiled the lady. 'And who would not, stuck in this damp place? Denied fine clothes, good wine, the company of gallants and a polite hand of whist? I am quite sure I would not find my temperament improved one whit if our positions were reversed.'

The Beadle glared at Molly, then looked at the lady. 'I don't —'

'I believe I have heard enough from you, Beadle,' said Emma Fairborn. 'Now then, Molly. Would you do me the favour of bringing me that book over there?'

Molly saw the leather-bound volume she was pointing to on one of the higher of the Beadle's bookshelves. She shrugged, walked over to the shelf and slid the book out. She blew the dust off the top. Pristine. Some work of philosophy kept for impressing visitors with the weight of the Beadle's intellect. Then she walked over to where the lady was sitting and passed the work across.

Damson Fairborn gently held Molly's hand for a second before turning it over and examining it like a gypsy palm reader. 'Thank you, Molly. I am so glad that your tenure in the employ of that Snell woman was brief. Your hands are far too nice to be ruined by bleach.' She placed the book down beside her. 'And you have a good sense of balance for someone with your height. A shade over five and a half feet I would say.'

Molly nodded.

'My dear, you have no idea how many pretty girls I meet who clump around like shire horses at a country fair, or waddle like a duck with the bad fortune to have been dressed in a lead corset. I think I can work with you. Tell me, Molly, have you enjoyed your time here at the house?'

'I have found it . . . somewhat wearisome, damson,' Molly replied.

She seemed amused. 'Indeed, have you? You have quite an erudite turn of phrase for someone raised between these walls.'

'The last director here was a Circlist, Damson Fairborn,' said the Beadle. 'She had the children in classes well past the statutory age, flouting the Relief of the Poor Act.'

'A mind is the hardest thing to improve and the easiest thing to waste,' said the lady. 'And you, Molly. You have received no salary for these labours, I presume?'

'No, damson,' Molly answered. 'It all goes to the Sun Gate Board of the Poor.'

Damson Fairborn nodded in understanding. 'Yes, I am sure I would be amazed at how expensive the ward's Victualling Board can buy in the cheapest kitchen slops. Still —' she looked directly at the Beadle '— I am sure the suppliers have their overheads.'

The Beadle positively squirmed behind his writing desk.

'Well, my dear.' Damson Fairborn adjusted the short silkprint wrap draped around her jacket's shoulders. 'You will do. I think I can pay you a handsome stipend once the poor board's monthly fees have been accounted for.'

Molly was shocked. If there was an employer who was paying the poorhouse's dole and adding on an extra salary for the boarders, it was a first for the Sun Gate workhouse. The whole rotten idea of the poorhouse was as a source of cheap labour for the ward.

'She's an orphan, mind,' reminded the Beadle. 'She reaches her maturity in a year and then she's a voter. I can only transfer her ward papers to you for twelve months.'

The lady smiled. 'I think after a year with me our young lady's tastes will be expensive enough that she won't wish to return to working for your Handsome Lane concerns.'

Molly followed her new employer out onto the street, leaving the dank Sun Gate workhouse to the Beadle and his minions. The lady had a private cab waiting for her, the horses and carriage as jet-black as the livery of the squat, bulletheaded retainer standing beside them.

'Damson Fairborn,' Molly coughed politely as the manservant swung open the cab door.

'Yes, my dear.'

Molly indicated the high prison-like walls of the poorhouse behind them. 'This isn't the usual recruiting ground for a domestic.'

Her new employer looked surprised. 'Why, Molly, I don't intend you for an undermaid or a scullery girl. I thought you might have recognized my name.'

'Your name?'

'Lady Fairborn, Molly. As in my establishment: Fairborn and Jarndyce.'

Molly's blood turned cold.

THE BLACK TATTOO
by Sam Enthoven
(Razorbill, $9.99)

Best friends Jack and Charlie inadvertently end up on opposite sides of a battle that will decide the fate of the universe. The two British lads are recruited by the Brotherhood of Sleep in hopes that they can assist in defeating the Scourge, an evil demon bent on destruction and domination. When Charlie becomes the vessel of the very force the group has sworn to battle, their parallel journeys send them to Hell and back, and Jack desperately tries to save not only the cosmos, but his friend as well.

THE MAGICAL LIFE
OF LONG TACK SAM
by Ann Marie Fleming
(Riverhead Books, $14)

Long Tack Sam was a magician and an acrobat in the early 20th century — a Chinese performer who toured the world as one of the most famous vaudeville acts of the day, but who has since been forgotten in the shadows of pop-culture history. In this unique illustrated memoir, Sam's great-granddaughter Ann Marie Fleming chases down the myriad contradictory myths about his life and tries to reconstruct the real story, however improbable.

SUMMER READING

WEIRDUCOPIA

THE RESURRECTIONIST
by Jack O'Connell
(Algonquin Books, $24.95)

Think Jasper Fforde meets *Lorenzo's Oil* meets *The Neverending Story*. In Jack O'Connell's incredible new novel, we meet Sweeney, a druggist whose son, Danny, has been left in a coma with minimal brain activity. Soon, however, Sweeney discovers that his son's condition is bizarrely linked to the comic-book universe of Limbo. Nurses, freaks, and magic converge as the author drives Danny and his father to their strange fate.

VICIOUS CIRCLE
by Mike Carey
(Grand Central, $24.99)

Mike Carey talked with *Weird Tales* last year (issue #346) about the debut of his ghost-hunting hero Felix Castor in *The Devil You Know*. Carey follows Castor back into his life of exorcism in the sequel, *Vicious Circle*, as the haunted protagonist takes some freelance paranormal work from the local police. One case threatens to be more than he can handle, sending Castor, his possessed friend Rafi, and the succubus Juliet on a quest to stop the reincarnation of a demon.

'Of course,' the lady winked at her heavily muscled retainer, 'Lord Jarndyce is sadly no longer with us. Isn't that so, Alfred?'

'A right shame, milady,' replied the retainer. 'Choked on a piece of lobster shell during supper, it was said.'

'Yes, Alfred. That was really rather careless of him. One of the very few occurrences of good living proving harmful to one's constitution, I should imagine.'

Molly's eyes were still wide with shock. 'But Fairborn and Jarndyce is —'

'A bawdyhouse, my dear. And I, not to place too delicate a sensibility on it, am widely known as the Queen of the Whores.'

The retainer stepped behind Molly, cutting off her escape route down the street.

'And you, Molly. I think you shall do very nicely indeed as one of my girls.'

BACK IN THE Beadle's office the Observer faded into the reality of the poorhouse. She was allowed only one intervention, and it had been one of her best. Small. As it had to be. Hardly an intercession at all.

Originally the Beadle had been intending to rent Molly's ward papers to the large abattoir over on Cringly Corner; but that reality path would have seen Molly returned, dismissed for insubordination, and back in the poorhouse within six weeks. Which would not have been at all beneficial for the Observer and her designs.

It had been so easy to nudge the Beadle's brain a degree to the side, letting the new plan form in his imagination. Harder to push Emma Fairborn's steel trap of a mind, but still well within the Observer's intervention tolerances. The Beadle was sitting behind his desk now, working out how much graft was due in by the end of the week.

The Observer made sure everything was tidy and accounted for in the man's treacle-thick chemical soup of a mind. Something, a sixth sense perhaps, made the Beadle scratch the nape of his neck and stare directly at where the Observer was standing. She increased the strength of her infiltration of his optic nerve, erasing even her background presence, comforting the small monkey brain back into a state of ease.

Silver and gold, think about the money. The Beadle shuffled his papers into a neat stack and locked them away in his drawer. It was going to be a good take again this week.

The Observer sighed and faded back out of reality. Sadly, the Beadle was not going to live long enough to purchase that twelfth cottage by the coast to add to his burgeoning property empire. She could have saved him. But then there were some interventions the Observer was glad she was not required to make. ☺

London-based author **Stephen Hunt** *currently serves on the management, technical, and editorial boards for SFcrowsnest.com, which is currently Google-ranked as the Internet's second most popular science-fiction Web site. The Court of the Air — acclaimed as a SCI FI Essential Book — is his second novel. It is available in bookstores in June.*

Lost in Lovecraft

A GUIDED TOUR OF THE DARK MASTER'S WORLD

BY KENNETH HITE

"*Why the beings and the sculptures lingered so late in the world, even until the coming of men, none can tell; unless it was because the land of Mnar is very still, and remote from most other lands, both of waking and of dream.*"

—H.P. Lovecraft,
"The Doom That Came to Sarnath"

FINDING THE "FIRST appearance" of Lovecraft's Dreamlands involves an appropriately murky exploration. For instance, his first three mature tales — "The Tomb," "Dagon," and "Polaris" — all involve dream visions that may or may not also be travel narratives. The first mention of "lands of dream" (a notion Lovecraft took from Dunsany, or perhaps from Winsor McKay?) in his fiction is in "The Doom That Came to Sarnath," but the only tale explicitly set in Dreamland is *The Dream-Quest of Unknown Kadath*. On the other hand, out of Lovecraft's fifty solo stories, thirty-nine feature or mention dreams, and five more mention nightmares. Of the six remaining, two — "The Cats of Ulthar" and "The Other Gods" — are conventionally considered "Dreamland" stories, though that convention dissolves if you examine it too closely. Just like Serranian, the "pink marble city of the clouds."

Leng, Kadath, Sarnath, and Lomar are all explicitly set in both Lovecraft's "real world" and in the Dreamland. Even Randolph Carter, the soul-symbol of the Dream Cycle, spends at least half his time in waking world adventures. The boundary between "Dreamland" stories and "Mythos" stories is so thin as to be risible. As thin, indeed, as one suspects Lovecraft considers the boundaries between the mundane world and any of his higher dimensions: the ultraviolet, hyperspace, the Dreamlands, the past of "He," or the chaos outside Erich Zann's window. Or, to be sure, the boundaries between life and death in "Cool Air" or

madness and reality in "Hypnos" or tale and truth in "Quest of Iranon" or man and monster in "Shadow Over Innsmouth" or science and blasphemy in "The Dunwich Horror." Thin-ness of boundaries, the lack of walls — of sleep or otherwise — seems to be a huge meta-concern spanning all of Lovecraft's work.

But back to Dreamland. Of fifty tales, by my count, only four have no connection with dreams. Further, Lovecraft drew elements of many of his stories, including "The Statement of Randolph Carter" and "Call of Cthulhu," from his own dreams. In a sense, Lovecraft's entire cosmos, from "changeless, legend-haunted" Arkham to the vaults of Zin, is a Dreamland.

"They reminded him, too, that not only had no man ever been to Kadath, but no man had ever suspected in what part of space it may lie; whether it be in the dreamlands around our own world, or in those surrounding some unguessed companion of Fomalhaut or Aldebaran. If in our dreamland, it might conceivably be reached . . . "

—H.P. Lovecraft,
The Dream-Quest of Unknown Kadath

Dreamland, meanwhile, is somewhere else. It is on the other side of the Gates of Deeper Slumber, and through a ghoul-burrow, and just that side of the Tanarian Hills, and through the Enchanted Wood. And that's just in one novel, the Dream-Quest. In "The White Ship," Basil Elton takes a White Ship across the Southern Sea to what might be Dreamland. King Kuranes of "Celephaïs" merely nods off and "journeys" there, although the specific "there" seems to vary with his age. The Dreamland is both the "inner world" and "around our world," and there are other "regions of dream" that aren't it at all. Dreamland has its own Moon and Saturn, at least, and there are other dreamlands entirely "surround-

(Center graphic: HANGING OUT IN DREAMLAND WITH A PRIOR KING)

ing some unguessed companion of Fomalhaut or Aldebaran." Parts of it resemble Earth — such as the patch of Cornwall dreamed into existence by Kuranes — and parts of it might even be on Earth, such as Randolph Carter's "sunset city," which he reaches not by falling asleep but by waking up.

"It was very strange, but as the riders went on they seemed to gallop back through Time . . . " —H.P. Lovecraft, "Celephaïs"

Perhaps more of Dreamland than we, or Randolph Carter, suspect lies on the Earth. Ulthar, for example, receives a visit from a young cat-fancier named Menes who (we are led to infer) will grow up to be that Menes who became the first Pharaoh of Egypt, dating the events of "The Cats of Ulthar" to approximately 3100 BC. Sarnath and Ib are explicitly dated to "ten thousand years ago," and in *At the Mountains of Madness,* Ib joins such faultlessly terrestrial locations as Atlantis, R'lyeh, Lomar, and Arabia's "nameless city." *At the Mountains of Madness* also incidentally further confounds the locations of Kadath and Leng, both occasional features of the Dreamland, by identifying them with the Old Ones' Antarctic conurbation. "The Other Gods" returns Kadath to such Dreamland environs as Hatheg-Kla, Ulthar, and so forth, but then sets them "in the youth of the world." Dreamland, in other words, is an ancestral memory-plane, or even the ancient world itself, as indeed Lomar (fl. 24,000 B.C.) turns out to be in "Polaris." In this context, it is perhaps significant that Lovecraft's commonplace-book story-seed for "Celephaïs" reads: "Man journeys into the past — or imaginative realm — leaving bodily shell be-

hind." And indeed, when Kuranes makes his final trip to Celephaïs, the riders escorting him seem "to gallop back through Time" past "houses and villagers such as Chaucer or men before him might have seen."

"Then he saw a sort of grey phosphorescence about, and guessed they were coming even to that inner world of subterrene horror of which dim legends tell, and which is litten only by the pale death-fire wherewith reeks the ghoulish air and the primal mists of the pits at Earth's core."

—H.P. Lovecraft,
The Dream-Quest of Unknown Kadath

But is Kuranes really traveling to the distant past on his final ride? It is, after all, his final ride because his hashish-stupefied "bodily shell" has fallen over an English cliffside somewhere. In short, Kuranes dies and goes to the Dreamlands. Something similar happens to Richard Upton Pickman, who is dragged into a tunnel in his Boston cellar only to emerge as a ghoul in the Dreamlands, a tough enough trick to manage even without adding time-travel to the mix. Barzai the Wise falls "into the sky" above Kadath, into a "damnable pit." George Wetzel's bravura essay "The Cthulhu Mythos" identifies the Dreamland directly with Hell, or rather with Elysium and Tartarus intermixed. The ghouls, and their vast piles of bones in the Vale of Pnath, usher in this hellish atmos-

Dreamland is on the other side of the Gates of Deeper Slumber, and it is also through a ghoul-burrow.

phere. Moreover, the Dreamlands of the Dream-Quest are full of "daemon" entities, "gargoyles," and other infernal signifiers, lurking in omnipresent pits, abysses, and gulfs. Like Dante's inferno, the way to the Dreamland lies both in the middle of a wood and in the "inner world." (Better yet, Mt. Ngranek lies within "the primal mists of the earth's core.") Like Avernus, one descends (770 steps) into Dreamland, although contra Virgil, the descent is not as easy as all that.

"A blessed haze lies upon all this region, wherein is held a little more of the sunlight than other places hold, and a little more of the summer's humming music of birds and bees; so that men walk through it as through a faery place, and feel greater joy and wonder than they ever afterward remember."

—H.P. Lovecraft,
The Dream-Quest of Unknown Kadath

Can these three Dreamlands be reconciled? Can the Dreamland be an amorphous parallel dimension, and the ancient past, and the pit of Tartarus all at once? What else might come from dreams and fancies, or the past, or Hell? A sampling of answers: According to the Edwardian anthropologist W.Y. Evans-Wentz, changelings are made while children are asleep. On the Isle of Skye, falling asleep on a fairy mound results in being taken to Fairyland. As the Irish author "A.E." put it: "Many go to the Tir-na-nog in sleep, and some are said to have remained there." Shakespeare's fairy encounters occur in an Enchanted Wood (zoog-free) during a midsummer night's dream.

So much for dreams. What of the past? The Irish *Book of Conquests* tells of the primordial Tuatha de Danaan, who retreated inside the hills to become the Daoine Sidh, or fairies, keeping their ancient world alive there. Lovecraft and Arthur Machen, among others, took this to mean that the "little people" were ancient survivals of a "Mongolian" race of pre-Britons. And Hell? Again, Evans-Wentz reports beliefs across the Celtic world

identifying the fairies with the spirits of the dead. The sluagh of the Highlands are the evil dead; Finvarra's troops in Ireland are likewise sinister sorts. Lady Wilde reports an Irish legend that the fairies are fallen angels. And of course Hell, Faërie, and Lovecraft's Dreamland are all underground realms.

Like Lovecraft's ghouls, fairies snatch trespassers and feed them a transforming food that keeps them in Fairyland forever. The merchants of Dylath-Leen, and the slavers from the Moon, and the nightgaunts, all likewise kidnap passersby in fine fairy style. The fate of Iranon in his eponymous quest resembles that of King Herla, who aged to dust upon return from Faërie. Like "Tir-na-nog," the fairies' Land of Youth, Ooth-Nargai holds "only perpetual youth." Sona-Nyl, where "there is neither time nor space," sounds like the eternal twilight realm of infinite meadows and forests tucked inside a fairy mound. The peculiar behavior of time and space in the Dreamland likewise tracks the tales of a night's dancing that lasts seven years, or of fairy rides across all England in a night. Dreamland and Fairyland overlap thoroughly, albeit mysteriously. Lovecraft read Machen and A.E., and the Anglo-Irish Lord Dunsany was of course familiar with the renaissance in Irish fairy lore that was occurring all around him. Exactly how the sidhe became the ghouls, or the redcaps the gugs, we may never know. But it seems as clear as the River Skai that whether by design, inspiration, or Dunsany, Lovecraft had discovered Fairyland, and dreamed himself its creator. ℮

Next Stop on the Tour: *The Pacific Ocean*

The Cryptic

PEOPLE: IT'S WHAT'S FOR DINNER

DOES THE NAME Sawney Bean mean anything to you, Gentle Reader? If so, it surely conjures up images of the darkest depths of human depravity and degeneracy, next to which Lovecraft's "decayed" New England Whateleys and Marshes are paragons of civic probity, although the Martense family in "The Lurking Fear" is a bit closer to the mark: inbred, dwarfish, half-human cannibals dwelling in caves and tunnels underneath an ancient mansion in the Catskills.

Indeed, cannibalism is the crux of the matter, because Sawney Bean (or Beane) and his extended family were the most famous cannibals in the history of Scotland. This is not to suggest that people eating people is a particularly common phenomenon in the north of Britain, and we will refrain from prying questions about what precisely is in that wonderful haggis they serve there, but Sawney Bean is something else again.

"The following account, though as well attested as any historical fact can be, is almost as incredible, for the monstrous and unparalleled barbarities that it relates," begins the "standard" version of the story, which tells how, some centuries ago, one Sawney Bean, the "idle" and generally ne'er-do-well son of a Scottish laborer, removed himself from respectable society in the company of a lady similarly inclined, and took up residence in caves in Galloway, where the happy couple was fruitful, multiplied astonishingly, and supported themselves entirely by highway robbery and cannibalism. So successful were they at this that they continued undetected for twenty-five years, as numerous travelers disappeared, several innocent innkeepers were hanged on suspicion of murder, and no one encountered the Bean family and did

other than "stay for dinner," even as the prolific clan increased incestuously unto a third generation. At last, a man and a wife, riding on the same horse on the way home from a fair, were attacked by the cannibals. The woman was dragged off the horse, butchered, her blood drunk "with great gusto" and her entrails were ripped in front of her husband's eyes. He fought bravely "with sword and pistol," knowing his fate would be the same, until a party of thirty more people returning from the same fair suddenly arrived on the scene. For the first time, someone had encountered the Bean clan and survived. Soon the king of Scotland himself, with four hundred armed retainers scoured the countryside, discovered the Beans' cave complex with its vast stores of smoked and picked human remains, and after a stout fight, all the cannibals were hauled off to Glasgow for edifyingly gory executions without any need for a trial. Not one of them repented, all screaming hideous curses to the end.

Such families of murderous rural cannibals have become a horror archetype, a sta-

The king of Scotland, with 400 armed men, captured the cannibal family and hauled them off for execution. Or so the tale goes.

92 ~ WEIRD TALES ~ July-August 2008

ple of the field. Among the novels on the subject are *The Flesh Eaters* by L.A. Morse (1979) and Guy N. Smith's *The Cannibals* (1986). Jack Ketchum's first book, *The Off Season* (1980) transplants the story to the Maine coast. Among film adaptations or films somewhat inspired by the story are Wes Craven's *The Hills Have Eyes* (1977, remade in 2006), *Evil Breed: The Legend of Samhain* (2003), *Hillside Cannibals* (2006), *Hotel Caledonia* (2008), which sets the story in the present day, and — although a less literal adaptation — *The Texas Chainsaw Massacre* (1974, remade in 2006).

So "well attested" and documented is the tale of the Bean clan that it turns up in any number of "true crime" books, including Jay Nash's *Encyclopedia of Crime* and *Almanac of World Crime*, C.E. Maine's *The World's Strangest Crimes*, and William Roughhead's *Rogues Walk Here*.

There is only one problem: not a word of this story is true.

I owe this insight to my friend and colleague Lee Weinstein, editor and writer and scholar par excellence. When I repeated the basic Bean story to him and insisted, "It's very well documented," he said, "Oh really? Show me."

Lee is a librarian by profession and an outstanding researcher who was once engaged by the editors of *Shocked and Amazed* to document the existence of "La Petomaine," an eccentric French performance artist whose, ahem, "talent" cannot be described delicately. (Look it up. That's why God made the Internet.) He also worked for a *National Enquirer* writer, carefully documenting each reported instance of human physiological oddities: cyclopses, "mermaids," two-headed babies, that sort of thing. Lee was the one who introduced me to Philadelphia's brilliantly weird Mutter Museum, with its world-class collection of bizarre medical specimens. Sawney Bean seemed right up his alley.

I have to confess that Lee did more of the research than I did, but I take credit for goading him on, and what we found out is quite instructive in showing how such stories assemble themselves and how you can take them apart again.

We began with the obvious question: Which king of Scotland? Various accounts cite a King James, sometimes James the First, but here we are already in difficulties, because this could mean either James the First of Scotland who ruled only part of the country between 1406 and 1437 (and did not control Galloway, where the Bean caves are "still to be seen" to this day; so he would not have been able to take an army there) or perhaps James the Sixth of Scotland who became James the First of England in 1603. In which case we're talking about Shakespeare's patron, for whom the Bard wrote Macbeth.

Okay — we've already got a spread of about 160 years here.

The next question was this: Why didn't Shakespeare or one of his contemporaries mention Sawney Bean? We followed this up with: Why isn't the "documentation" even better? The life of James VI a.k.a. James I, the first Stuart king of Great Britain, is exceptionally well chronicled. You would think that if he had participated in something as shocking as an armed raid on a clan of cannibals, and had personally presided over all those dismemberments and burnings afterwards, which were carried out in fully public view in Glasgow (Edinburgh by some accounts), this would have, in effect, made the evening news. People would talk about it. Writers would mention it. It would become proverbial. There would be lurid ballads written, and maybe an even more lurid play on the order of Thomas Kyd's *The Spanish Tragedy*, the 16th century equivalent of a slasher flick.

But there is silence. Almost.

We found a very old "Historie of Scotland" by Robert Lindsay of Pitscottie (circa 1532-1578) which reports strange portents marking the death of James the Second (1460) including a "blazing star," the birth of

ILLUSTRATION BY STEVEN ARCHER

a hermaphrodite, and, incidentally, "a certaine theefe" who lurked in "a den in Angus called Fenisden," where he and his family robbed and ate passers-by, until finally caught, whereupon all the family was burnt at the stake. One daughter was spared, she being only a year old at the time, but by the time she was twelve she displayed similar appetites and met the same fate.

The story is repeated in Raphael Holinshed's *Chronicles of England, Scotland, and Ireland* (1577). This is the same Holinshed that Shakespeare used as a source for several of his plays.

This looked like paydirt, but it was not definitive. The Lindsay/Holinshed version does not mention Sawney Bean by name, nor does it contain the heroic husband and the disemboweled lady on her way home from the fair. Holinshed was not noted for extreme accuracy, which is one reason why many Shakespeare history plays only slightly resemble the actual reality of the events they depict. There is also, clearly, an oral tradition at work here. Note that the daughter who was spared only to reveal her evil nature has been dropped from later versions.

All this was very tantalizing, but it did not prove the case. That was where, in the course of our researches, the matter rested. The standard version of the Sawney Bean story — the one quoted above, "as well attested as any historical fact can be" — seems to have appeared in the English sensational press about 1730 under the byline of Captain Charles Johnson, which some scholars think to be a pseudonym of Daniel Defoe, the author of *Robinson Crusoe*.

The early 1700s were a golden age of sleazy journalism in England, a time of quickie pamphlets and broadsides which were the equivalent of today's supermarket tabloids. There are lots of mentions of Sawney Bean from that period. But just because something is in print doesn't make it true, then or now. The Johnson version found its way into John Nicholson's *Historical and Traditional Tales Connected with the*

Darrell Schweitzer is senior contributing editor to *Weird Tales* and *H.P. Lovecraft's Magazine of Horror.*

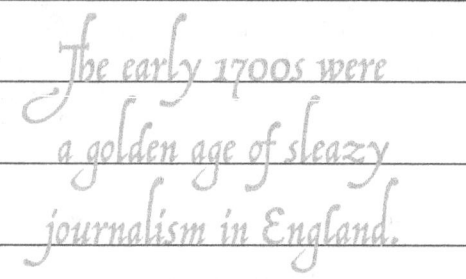

The early 1700s were a golden age of sleazy journalism in England.

South of Scotland (1843), from which it was included in the widely reprinted and very common landmark anthology *The Omnibus of Crime* (1934) edited by none other than Dorothy L. Sayers of Lord Peter Whimsey fame. Most mystery or horror fans have this book in their libraries.

The Newgate Calendar, another popular 18th-century compendium perhaps comparable to *The Encylopedia of Crime* or *Serial Killers from A to Z*, tells us that Sawney Bean's original first name was Andrew and that he was born in East Lothian in the 16th century.

There was still something wrong with this picture. The story could not be quite connected back to its alleged source. The literature of the 17th century is curiously silent on the matter. That the story seems to shift around both in time and in place (in some versions Galloway becomes Galway, in Ireland) is a sure sign of what would today be called an "urban legend," i.e. a folktale, improved with the telling, whispered from person to person until its source has been forgotten.

Or it might even be a slander against Scotsmen. Remember that the early 17th century was the time of the Jacobite uprisings (Bonnie Prince Charlie and all that) and that the English of the day tended to view Scots as dangerous and barbaric. So why not cannibalistic too? Isn't it to be expected of wild men in kilts who come screaming out of the fog-shrouded highlands to lop your head off with their enormous claymores?

Finally, Lee and I discovered that all our work had been done for us already, and that Ronald Holmes had written an entire book on

The Legend of Sawney Beane (Frederick Muller, Ltd, 1975). This covers everything: the legend, Sawney Bean in literature, such documentation that there is, the question of which king of Scotland, Galloway vs. Galway, folk beliefs on ogres, prehistorical cannibalism, and much more. Holmes even brings up an objection we hadn't thought of, which is that if you do the math and figure out how old Sawney Bean and his wife must have been and how long it would take Mrs. Bean to give birth to the attested eight sons and six daughters and for them to produce eighteen grandsons and fourteen granddaughters (not counting stillbirths and early childhood mortalities caused by the filthy conditions inside the cave), Papa Bean must have been presiding over a cannibal nursery. Most of the Beans would have been children.

Nutritionists have also calculated that, in order to support that many people for that long by cannibalism alone, the Beans would have had to have eaten the entire population of southern Scotland.

Sure enough, the name "Sawney" was once a derogatory term for a Scotsman. Very likely, then, the story was made up, or at least developed, to exploit English fears of the "wild Scots" in the popular mind circa 1730. From there it spread out. Once the political context was forgotten, the Scots somehow came to embrace the story as a colorful piece of their folklore.

When I took a ghost tour of Edinburgh in 1995, the guide solemnly repeated the whole, ghastly tale. It was not a place to express doubts. That would have spoiled the fun.

So one of the standard horror icons came out of, almost, nowhere. There might have been a basis in oral tradition, but there is none in history. The spectacular parts of the tale — the involvement of the Scottish king with his army and the mass, public executions of the Bean clan — cannot be found in history at all. But the power of the image remains.

One lesson we drew from this is that "true crime" books tend to repeat "facts" from other "true crime" books and, without really good references, should not necessarily be taken any more seriously than the average UFO book. Another is that when the story is good enough and ghastly enough, mere facts (or the lack thereof) do not much matter. And therefore one thing about the sordid tale *is* certain: We have not heard the last of Sawney Bean. ℮

From the author of
Mélusine and *The Virtu*

THE DEAD AND THE MONSTROUS WILL NOT LEAVE KYLE MURCHISON BOOTH ALONE.

"SARAH MONETTE CAN WRITE LIKE A DREAM."
—CHARLAINE HARRIS

SARAH MONETTE

the Bone Key

THE NECROMANTIC MYSTERIES OF KYLE MURCHISON BOOTH

One nervous antiquities scholar . . . ten tales of the supernatural.

Available now from Prime Books

WWW.THEBONEKEY.COM

'The 85 Weirdest Storytellers of the Past 85 Years'

Our 85th anniversary feature last issue drew more attention than any other story in WT's modern history. Here's a sampling ~ there's more at WeirdTalesMagazine.com!

You Loved 'em

That is an incredible list. I love that Warren Zevon and Kate Bush both get mentions. —*Grant Stone*

Wonderful, concise write-up of Clark Ashton Smith's contribution to weird fiction. It is nice to see that he is getting more of the attention that he so rightly deserves. —*Colin Azaria-Kribbs*

I was quite startled to find some of the selections here, but I can't find myself disagreeing with many of them. I'm glad Thomas Ligotti is acknowledged. He deserves a wider readership outside of his small but loyal cult following. *Weird Tales* has done a great deal to support his work over the years, and fortunately, it appears you will continue to do so. —*The Grim Blogger*

Joyce Carol Oates is the greatest living American writer. Period. And Laurie Anderson is a genius! —*Elle Reasoner*

Douglas Adams's clever and puckish use of the English language is sadly underrated. I think there's more to learn about the artful use of words from Adams's trick of twisting clichés and subverting expectations over the course of a sentence than from a truckload of ponderous dystopic novels. —*Pauline J. Alama*

Mervyn Peake beats Mr. Tolkien & Mr. Lewis hands down in style, character development, sensitivity to people different from himself, locale, and sheer imaginative gusto. And all without the creepy misogyny/racism of the other two. —*Matthew Pridham*

Roald Dahl's adult fiction is just as macabre as his children's stories. He is the master of the twist-in-tale, and manages to capture the darker side of human nature with comical, effortless ease. —*James Harris*

We Missed 'em

Good list, but I would have liked to have seen Fritz Leiber, Karl Edward Wagner, Frank Frazetta, and Christopher Lee make the cut too. —*Manfred Arcane*

Great list. Of course we must add Borges, probably the Brothers Quay, Guy Maddin, Henry Darger, and perhaps Bruno Schultz. Also, what about Gary Gygax? —*Peter Harkness*

No Jack Kirby? No Walter Simonson? No Salman Rushdie? No Gene Wolfe? Great list, though. 85 is obviously too few to please everyone. Nice to see that people weren't too snobbish to include Stephen King and Dr. Seuss. —*Sean Gilroy*

Ingmar Bergman. Alfred Hitchcock. Federico Fellini. Kathy Acker. Jorge Luis Borges. Gertrude Stein. Carol Emshwiller. Queensryche. Blue Oyster Cult. —*Mike Allen*

Where is Caitlín R. Kiernan? Surely she deserves to be on this list? She's written some of the best "weird" this side of Lovecraft! —*Magan Rodriguez*

I would love to add Diane Arbus, who took photographs of human pincushions, headless women, children with toy hand grenades, giants, dwarves, cross-dressers, and the mentally challenged. —*Allison Rich*

I can think of few writers of the last eighty-five years who could equal Robert Aickman in terms of undiluted unapologetic weirdness. On the painting front, Dali but no Magritte? Surely a purer surrealist. And David Lynch certainly deserves his listing, but I would have thought his great predecessor in the cinema of surrealism does too: Luis Bunuel. —*Ramsey Campbell*

I was surprised that Frank Zappa wasn't included, especially since several musicians were. All in all, though, an interesting, far-ranging list of names. Well done. —*Greg L. Johnson*

www.ingramcontent.com/pod-product-compliance
Lightning Source LLC
Chambersburg PA
CBHW082016170626
46817CB00009B/3112